THE MIDNIGHT CONVERSATIONS OF FREUD AND PLATH...

MAALU...

The people who came to my life...

Who taught me lessons and gave me memories to
cherish...

Contents

Contents

Contents

PREFACE

All the characters mentioned are purely fictional. Any resemblance to the existing people is coincidental.

I

Conversation One...

She lit her cigarette with her metal lighter... The metal... cold against her scarred fingers... It was a gift... She remembered... But from whom... She didn't remember that... The cigarette butt giving out a warm glow...

She then looked out of the window... into the dark cold night... the smoke... slowly but severely burning her throat and her insides...

"What are you thinking...?" asked a voice... a voice she's grown too familiar of... too familiar that it doesn't threaten her when he abruptly throws his words at her...

She let out the smoke as a reply... words weren't that important... with him... words simply didn't matter... They could know... deep down... they could feel...

"... only if you're okay..." he added... if that addition was too important...

"Darkness..." She whispered... barely audible to him... If he hadn't noticed her thin line of lips... he would've almost missed it... "... is spread out like a blanket... heavy only to those who can feel it... and for the rest... nothing much..." a long silence... He knew better not to interrupt... He waited...

waited in such a way that if he hadn't blinked at times... it would seem like he was a statue... even his breathing paused... silently...

"... do you think it's coincidence that I feel darkness is heavy...?"

"I don't know... I've never felt it heavy..."

She blinked a few times... not daring to look at him... pretending that it was the smoke that caused tears in her eyes...

"Why's it heavy for you...?" he asked... and she knew... he asked it out of habit... even when he knew the answer to it... asked it only to hear it from her own lips...

"I'm not sure... it weighs down on me like a heavy blanket... crushing my bones... forcing me to scream... It makes me want to cry... even though there's nothing much going on in my life... but... I guess... it's because of all the secrets that I keep... that's weighing down on me... and all the faces of those... who never understood me... or my past..."

"I guess..." He replied... unmoving... not even twitching... If one didn't actually paid attention... one wouldn't hear his breath... It made her wonder... if he was an assassin in disguise...

"Plath..." he whispered as if recollecting her name out of a blank space... "... sometimes... it's usual to feel everything heavy... everything weighing down on us... forcing us to bend our knees and beg for forgiveness..." another deep pause as if he was brooding on the last word... considering every syllable of it... She waited for him to speak... Seconds... Minutes... But it seemed that he was done...

And then she finally looked at him... and he was smiling... assuring her that it's all going to be fine... and the cigarette she'd lit... groaned barely in the cold wind that

MAALU...

brushed past the corner of her eyes...

***

• 3 •

II

Conversation Two...

She was reading a book... her legs dangling from one side of the armrest of the chair she sat in... careless and unbothered of any womanly manners... He walked in from the bedroom with dishevelled hair and a ghost of a yawn that he'd tried to suppress... or maybe swallow in an effort to keep his sleep at bay... Both of them... he remembered... had slept late... And yet... she was up and about reading... while he fell asleep some time in the evening... Looking outside... he could see the darkness of the night...

"Do you think sensing each other's presence is part of being a soulmate...?" she'd asked out of blue as he was preparing himself some dinner... He knew she wasn't a cook... but she was always better at it than yesterday...

"Did I interrupt...?" he asked...

"No... not really..." she whispered barely audible... He knew she'd do it... this whispering when she's lost somewhere else... "Your presence doesn't actually interrupt..." He noticed... she'd her eyes glued onto the pages... her fingers carefully placed under the line she's paused for now... searching for something in between the

"

lines...

"Do you really believe in soulmates...?" he asked after careful thought...

She responded with a sigh... and then the sound of shutting the book with a bookmark in between... Her hand... he watched... was still on the book... but now over the cover page... *Wuthering Heights*... he read...

"I guess..." she replied... not looking at him... then she sighed again... now... finally turning to look at him... but actually looking beyond him... He noticed... how she could always see beyond what he was... what his body was... It frightened him at times... and at most times... he got lost in them... her chocolate brown eyes...

"I don't think finding a random person from the street and making things work between us will actually work for me..."

He knew... he was like her too... in that sense... He threw a ball of grape into his mouth... and savoured the sour taste... He watched her longingly... still as he could be... except for his calculated moves of his hands... and the movement of his mouth as he chews down his food...

"I guess... the madness is burnt right into our souls the day our souls were born... and believing in soulmates was part of that madness..." he replied soon after he'd gulped down his food... It was a task to keep his thoughts locked and hidden from her... It demanded to fall from his lips...

She blinked at him... and sighed once more... as if to say... she was satisfied with the answer... but her eyes seemed to betray her... They were still on some complicated thoughts... and there were more questions to come...

"Do you think we'll realise when we meet our soulmates...?"

He thought for a while and then smiled tilting his head in a neat angle... some gesture she loved to watch... All his gestures... she thought... had mathematical precisions even when he claimed he was weak at it...

"I realised you... when I met you..."

She tilted her head smiling... trying to imitate him... but it was never mathematically precise like his...

"What about multiple soulmates...?"

"I don't know about that... I've never had that much of a social life..."

She silently sank back to the chair thinking... Maybe that was better... She should've waited too... rather than running around and finding too many lovers... At random times... she felt impure... but that was another conversation to worry about...

"Freud...?"

"Mmm...?"

"Do you think soulmates forgive each other for their past sins...?"

"..." It was utter silence that for a moment she thought he'd vanished into thin air... "Yes... Mistakes are never sins... they're just mistakes... that's all... and mistakes are meant to be forgiven..."

He heard her sigh again... this time genuinely... and he smiled at the thought of her breath lingering behind in that room where he existed too...

***

III
Conversation Three...

They were sitting on beanbags reading their own books... one of her feet outstretched towards his naked chest while his feet were somewhere close to her knees... She shut the book rather suddenly that was the only sound in that 'pin drop silence' room...

"Freud..." she called out of the blue... and he smiled to the pages he was reading and lifted his sight towards her with yet another tilt that she fell in love by now...

"..." Everything was in his smile... she knew... that's how they had their silent conversations for so long...

"What do you love the most... love poems or love letters...?" His smile widened... ear to ear... on hearing her question and she watched as his pupils jerked towards the upper corner of his eyes as if he was putting serious thought into the question... His hands on the other hand... they were moving calculatedly... those strong fingers placing the bookmark in between...

"It doesn't matter... as long as it's from you..." He said after a long pause... looking at her chocolate brown eyes and grinning from ear to ear... something he'd done only with her...

She stared... not replying... not sighing a satisfaction to the answer... and he smiled once more...

"You aren't satisfied...!" He told more to himself than to her... But then again... it didn't matter... Their souls were blended beyond boundary that he was her and she was him...

"For me... it never mattered as long as it's from you... But if you're really pressing on it... I'd prefer love poems..."

It was her turn to jerk her pupils to the corner of her eyes and brood... "Why...?" She asked staring at that invisible marvel that lingered in the corner of their room... her fingers tracing the texture of the book cover in an absent-minded manner...

"Your poems... they're quite normal poems from the surface... but a riddle as I read it again and again... Like a puzzle piece... that I've full liberty to fix somewhere... some place it fit... and create a picture I want..."

She still didn't sigh her satisfaction... and a small chuckle... or more like a phantom of a chuckle escaped his lips...

"And yet... I'd rather choose to fix those puzzle pieces with you... Not in a way I want... but in a way we want..."

She sighed now... sinking back to her beanbag... her leg still outstretched towards his chest... He squeezed her feet as an assurance and she went back to reading... which he watched smiling for a whole of five minutes... and then he too... went back to his book...

***

IV
Conversation Four...

It rained outside... a least expected rain... The night seemed to grow darker and she didn't think night could grow much darker than it already was... She stared at the pouring rain... hugging herself tighter towards her... and quite unexpectedly she felt a soft... warm blanket sliding over her shoulders and wrapping around her with a much warmer body inside with her... She smiled more to herself... knowing clearly who it was as his warm, strong hand wrapped around her shoulder... the blanket tightly wrapped... not letting even a sliver of cold air to slip towards her already frozen skin...

"Plath..." he murmured... breaking the silence at its core... "Do you think we were meant to meet in this world...?" The words seemed to slip out with much difficulty and she felt he was at one of his moments of insecurity... where he is adamant that someday... she's going to vanish from his life into thin air... leaving him alone...

"Mmm...?"

"You know... like... do you think we were meant to meet in this life... like a predestined fate... like a plan made by God... or something...?"

"Ah...!" She whispered more to herself... signalling him that she's got that clarification of the question he was trying to spit out... She stared into the distance... her mouth gaping a bit... as if she was sucking in the cold air... to warm herself... She then... without a warning... looked into his eyes... He was familiar with her unpredictability... Once... in an attempt to look at him all of a sudden... she'd twisted her neck so quickly... the pain almost brought her to tears... He'd always wondered what the hurry was... like she did that twisting so quickly as if she was afraid... he might leave if she were slow... But he wasn't going anywhere...

"I'm not going to vanish into thin air..." She whispered as if she'd looked into his eyes and seen something way beyond his eyes... probably his soul... and all those thoughts that rummaged and churned inside his brain...

"And for the question you asked..." She once again looked away... into the distance... and smiled to herself... as if she'd read something from the strong tree trunk... of the tree that stood opposite to where they sat... "We were meant to cross paths... We were meant to... run into each other... speak up words we've never said to anyone before in our lives... You... taking all the initiative you've never taken before and wishing me a Good Morning... and me... going wide eyed at that very instant... because no one wished me that before... Yes... I guess we were meant to meet... in this world..."

He sighed... in satisfaction... and more as a relief... His grip on her shoulder tightened in assurance... and then went gentle as before... But he'd questions... more questions...

"Why do you think... we met...?" His voice had gone hoarse... and it seemed a mighty effort to ask...

"You tell me..." she said smiling at him... one of her hands softly placed on his knee... "You've always told me... none had understood you... none had read you... the way I've... You tell me... why we met..."

He knew... he smiled... She smiled back in answer... He knew the answer so well... but it was reassuring to hear from her lips...

"We met because..." She began as if she read his mind... "... we were lonely for so long... we were left lonely and complicated enough that none could actually understand us... that finally we had to meet... so that someone in this huge ocean of a world... could actually solve a riddle that's you... and could solve me in return..." She squeezed his knee in assurance and he watched her glitter painted nails... He traced the curves of her fingers with his... and it was assurance enough for him... that she existed right then and there... and that she was there with him right then and there... and that she wasn't going anywhere... not yet... not ever... It was magical enough... and almost like a fantasy... that both of them existed solely for each other... Him for her... and her for him... Finally met... finally right there... and finally spending their days together... in such stability... and such assurance and calmness... that both of them... never felt before...

***

V
Conversation Five...

She lit her cigarette with that same metallic lighter that she used each time... the smoke rising out of her gently gaping mouth... watching the darkness cloud the whole hemisphere of the earth... She could feel a presence behind her... not strong enough to distract... but powerful enough to let her know... It was more like a choice... like a decision he made... if he wanted her to know his presence... or not...

"Mmm...?" She hummed a question at him... still looking outside... the puff of smoke gently rising to the darkened skies to paint it grey...

"Why do you smoke...?" He asked... She could feel his eyes fixed on the back of her head... assessing what she thought... what went through that brain...

"I thought you were all about *everyone had their own choices* kind of person...?" She shot back... and immediately regretted it... but she didn't apologise... she wasn't ready...

"I'm still on that..." He whispered... Somewhere in his trembling voice... hurt lingering behind... "I wanted to know *why*...?"

She understood... understood what he was aiming at... She took as much as she can of that grey... burning smoke into her... and puffed it out into a huge cloud... that seemed like a cloud of misfortune revolving around her head... about to rain down any time soon...

"I wanted to burn all my impurities out..." She whispered barely audible to him... She simply looked at the glowing butt of the cigarette... thinking if she should crush down the half-devoured cigarette... or not... She wondered why he hadn't replied her yet... She desperately wanted to see what he was doing... but didn't feel like turning around... Not yet... not now...

"Who told you..." there was a pause... a short... but heavy pause... "... that you're impure...?"

She sighed... deeply... Not the one that told him that she was satisfied... but the one that told him she was exhausted... mostly of explaining it multiple times... to multiple people... expecting them to understand... at least a fraction of what she did for them...

"Everyone says so... every single person..." She whispered... And he could feel... she meant her family as well...

"Why do you think they're right...?" He asked... He didn't know if it was the right question... but too much of these questions made him feel that he has turned into a counsellor asking questions to his patient... making her find her own answers...

"Because they're right... I've had... too many..." There was a pause... He knew... he filled her blanks quite often... and not once had he been wrong... "... too many for my own good..." She added... with such difficulty that her voice trembled... and he could feel she was crying...

"I feel like hugging you..." He whispered... a silence seeking for her consent... She knew... and he knew she knew it too...

"I would love that..." She whispered... her voice trembling much more... He went up to her... and she let him guide her course of action as he took out her cigarette and popped it out into the ash tray... as he held both her shoulders with both his hands and turned her towards her... and hugged her close to his chest... but being equally tall... she reached somewhere around his neck and shoulders... She muffled her face deeper into him and started whimpering uncontrollably... like a little child... and he could feel her frame shaking... and his neck getting wet with her tears... as they ran down his neck to his chest... making their way to his heart...

"You're not... impure..." He whispered on top of her head... his one hand on the back of her head... and the other behind her... just below her shoulders... "What others say... it's not true... Everyone goes through this... You barely had any choices..."

"But... you... you... never went through... this..." He could feel the trembling and the breaking of her words as she whispered into his neck... fresh hot tears making their way to his heart...

"I'd a choice... you didn't..." He whispered... his grip on her tightening... but still gentle...

"I chose to be with them..."

"I don't think it was much of a choice... It was more of a survival choice... It's different from the normal choice..."

"I let him break me... just because I chose..."

"You chose me... It was his choice as much as it was mine... You're not at fault... He's..."

She cried... literally... as if she was pouring all her pain out... like she was crying for the first time in her entire life... or at least... if she was crying wholly for the first time...

"You're not impure... Don't let others tell you otherwise... They don't know who you're... They don't know your choices... They don't know your life... They never knew you... They... they only saw your outcomes... You can't judge a person with that... That's like judging based on a comparison of mystery book with a science fiction... They're entirely different although they might look similar..."

She finally stopped trembling... and lifted her head slightly... as if she was assessing the mess she created on his neck and chest... The cool wind sends a shiver down the path her tears had travelled...

"I'm sorry..." She whispered...

"Never be sorry for crying..." He kissed her forehead gently... and she smiled to his neck... as he wiped away her tears... Some words and their meanings are always irrelevant when it came to the mistaken past... if their futures were indeed corrected... they both knew it... they both have gone through it...

***

VI

Conversation Six...

Somewhere in the background a music plays... Ed Sheeran sings lines from *Photograph*...

"Loving can heal...

Loving can mend your soul...

And it's the only thing that I know, know..."

It was his favourite song... She knew... He'd made her sing before... And though... not a singer... she has sung the song many a times for him... Again... her lips move along the lines... those lines that have etched in her heart... and he was listening to her voice... barely audible over Ed Sheeran...

"I love it more when you sing..." He said... his smile plastered on his lips... She raised her eyes from the book in which she was doodling and smiled to him...

"You're the only person who would tell me that... that I'm better than Ed Sheeran..." She said rolling her eyes...

"Isn't it enough...?"

She looked at him once more... a mischievous smile playing on her lips... "Yes it's..." She assured... But it seemed that something was left hanging... something more to come... "... Freud...?"

"Mmm...?"

"Do you think love heals us...?"

His pupils went to a corner... as if he was thinking... She loved watching him think... a little genius considering even her silliest questions...

"I do... Love does heal... But..." He left it hanging... and then looked into her eyes... "... but it depends on the person..." There was a huge pause... and then his eyes had an entirely different expression... which only she could read out of that still... calm face... "What do you think... Plath...?"

She was taken aback by the question... which she didn't think would come back to her... It was her turn to consider... Her mouth gently opened... her eyes still fixed on an invisible spot out in the darkened skies... "I think..." she then turned her head quickly to see him better... to look into his eyes better... "I think it's the person who heals themselves... Love... it just acts as a catalyst... You know..." Another pause... She was terrible at talking... just as he... She found it difficult to find the right words when she spoke... She always did a better job at writing... "... you know... the healing... it's a tough process... you need support... a pillar of support... a shoulder to lean on... that's what love gives... a shoulder... a strong hand... Healing... that's something the person has to do... And we... we just hold onto their hands... tell them they're doing a good job... let them know they aren't alone... that we've got their back... Love doesn't heal... Love only helps..."

He smiled... He knew she was going to say the exact idea of love even before she began... He knew... and still he asked... It was always beautiful to make her speak...

Somewhere in the background... *Photograph* had left... and only those lines of a song that he's heard her sing before... but a song whose name nor singer he knew of...

popped up...

"When the sun shine, we shine together...
Told you I'll be here forever...
Said I'll always be your friend...
Took an oath and I'm stick it out till the end...
Now that it's raining more than ever...
Know that we still have each other...
You can stand under my umbrella...
You can stand under my umbrella..."

And the lines... simply merged and faded away... in her voice that joined along...

***

VII

Conversation Seven...

She was staring at her wrist... like she was lost in a trance... Trance seemed a beautiful word... but not apt to describe her condition... He knew what she was staring at... he could see... and even without looking... he could guess... The scars that made their way on her wrist...

"Why do we've scar...?" She asked out of blue... as if noticing his eyes glued into her wrist... just like hers was...

"All those... every single one of it... It's because of me... isn't it...?"

"No..." There was a huge pause... and he felt she was lying for the first time... He was adamant that it was because of him... because of him who kept thinking that it was better to walk away... whenever his insecurities popped up... "... my scars... they're never because of any person in particular... It's not because of any person actually..."

He knew... there was no place for him... no further questions to ask... He knew... She'd to tell... on her own time...

"... it's... it's because of the pain... not being able to connect with anyone... and finally... finally when you thought you made that final click... they just..." she whispered... barely audible... her voice trembling...

"I don't have a role in your life... do I...?" he asked... more out of habit than he had intended...

"... finally felt like I made that click... and then just... snap... It's that easy... for everyone...?" she asked if she hadn't actually heard the question...

"It's not for me... it's not my fate..." he whispered... more to himself than to her...

"You know... when I began hating having money...?"

"..."

"... the day I realised that money can buy you the best mother and father that you want... and before that money... blood relation is nothing but a hoax... and I'm tired... of pretending that everything is fine... because my mother doesn't look into my eyes... my father trusts my mother blindly... which is a good thing for her... but for me... I'm an orphan by definition... but not physically so no one will adopt me... and for once... I thought... I'd... I'd..." She began falling into fits of tears... shaking uncontrollably as she cried... going breathless... and he... for once... he got so afraid... he literally took large leaps towards her... where she sat on her favourite beanbag... He kneeled down... and held her hands tightly... his hands wrapping around her tiny palms... He had no words... words would only make it worse... they could... after all... communicate without words...

He knew... as he looked into her eyes... She wasn't crying for one reason at a time... but massive number of reasons... beginning from her childhood... her unhealed trauma... her inner child crying for her parents to come back... begging them to look at her... hug and kiss her... Her desperate attempts to get a mother... at least for a few days... someone... anyone... Her desperate attempts to find someone who actually understood her... for what she is... and for who she is... And her crying... screaming at all the Gods she believed in to have someone to confide in not feeling that she's a burden to them... someone who wouldn't leave... no matter what... no matter how hard both their life gets... and she could just melt right now... and bury herself in the earth... if she knew how to...

"Can I kiss you...?" He asked... and she blinked at him... breathing hard... her face reddened too much that he feared that her face would burst open...

"Can I kiss you...?" He repeated again... and she nodded...

"I need consent..." He replied... daring to smile at her... a risk he was ready to take...

"Yes..." she said smiling... or at least trying to... and he bend down... another mathematical move... as he turned her hand... exposing the scars on her wrist... and kissed on them gently... and he could feel... all her tears bursting open once again... not because she was sad this time... but because she was finally home... a place she could trust...

***

VIII
Conversation Eight...

"Are you asleep...?" He asked as he was running his fingers in her hair as she lied on his chest... listening to his heart beat... her voice slow... and calm... as if she'd slept...

"No..." She said as she inhaled all of him... his presence... his scent... His wholeness...

"Can I ask you something serious...?" He asked...

"Yes..." She replied... her fingers spiralling around the hairs on his chest... feeling the smoothness of it...

"Why is it that love makes my heart ache... like my fear that I'll lose you... keeps me awake at times..."

She raised her head all of a sudden and stared at his eyes... She leaned in and kissed him on his chin and she smiled... going back to lying down on his chest...

"You've your arm around me... how would you lose me...?"

"I don't know... I feel like somebody or something would take you away from me... the fear that when finally... I'd someone to understand me and love me as much as I do now... I feel you'll be lost... Somebody or something will take you away from me..."

"I'm afraid too... at times..." She confessed... He'd never seen her worried about that particular fear... "I'm afraid at times... But... I love you anyway... I find my happiness in it anyway... I love you for I love you..."

"How can you do that...?"

"I don't know..." She whispered... her breath cooling his chest... "I guess you learn it together... to love no matter what... to love to the very last breath..."

"I wish I were like that too... like you..." And he hugged her tighter... trying to make her stay...

"You'll learn... You'll learn with me... until we both die... until we both merge as a single soul... until we both stop merging..."

And with that... they both closed their eyes... and the night stole them away on the chariot of sleep...

***

IX
Conversation Nine...

She was lying on his chest... her short hair spread all over his chest... listening to music... one of the ear pieces in her ear and the other in his... The Tamil version of their song was playing in the track... and she was humming to the song... his fingers running through her hair...

"Freud...?" She called out of the blue... breaking the silence that lingered around... other than the song that kept playing...

"Mmm...?" She could feel his chest vibrate as he hummed... She felt calm... listening to his breathing... feeling the ups and downs of his chest... feeling his fingers at the top of her forehead...

"Why don't we fit in this world... like others... like normal people do...?" She stared at the ceiling as if hoping to get an answer from there... somehow...

"I don't know..." He said... and there was a huge pause... He stared at the ceiling too... expecting some answer from it... "... I guess... we're not meant for this world... or at least... we were born late... you know... old souls..."

She sighed deeply... old souls... she knew what it meant... "How do these old souls survive...?" She asked... her fingers interlocking with his fingers of his free hand...

"I guess..." he said... his fingers tightening around hers... in an easy gentle grip... "... they end up belonging to each other... wholly..."

She turned her head to face him and he lowered his gaze to meet her eyes... they kissed each other... with their eyes... and smiled... with their heart...

***

X

Conversation Ten...

Her favourite conversations always happened right after their love making... where they've merged spiritually... on a dimension that's beyond the third dimension... She was lying on the bed... staring at the ceiling... his head peacefully rested on her breast... He was listening to her heartbeat that was slow and calm... and her breathing was rough on the edges... tired and almost sleepy...

"Freud...?" She called out of the blue... her fingers running through his soft hair strands... her other hand resting over his bicep... her fingers circling on the curves of his bicep... that has wrapped around her...

"Hmm...?" His chest vibrated against her... sending goose-bumps down her spine...

"Am I being selfish...?"

He raised his head and looked into her eyes... He could see traces of pain in them... His eyes enquired what she meant by that question...

"For wanting to be loved... for wanting a person to love me... to celebrate my existence... to feel lucky just because I exist... to love me so wildly... so beautifully... in all planes...

and not just on physical terms... but on all levels... something that's quite metaphysical... for wanting to be cherished... simply for existing and existing alone...?"

The silence grew heavy between them... and in that silence... she could feel... he was thinking... looking for the right words... for he... at times... said words that didn't actually fit in... and this time... he didn't want to do it... he wanted to make it perfect... and thus... he was looking for the right words...

"I don't think so..." He said... and then again... a pause... "... wanting to be loved the way you love others... wholly and completely... it's basic need... and it's the most relevant need as well... I know... we both have been wanting that same kind of love... and I know... I've you to love me like that... feeling lucky just because I exist... so unconditionally... so beautifully... so aesthetically... as if I'm your poetry... as if I'm your art... and I don't know what I did to deserve you... I'm glad for I've met you..." And he kissed over her heart... his lips meeting with her already sweaty skin... "... and I know... your heart has broken a million times... and you've stitched them back as good as you could... and I know those stitches have been torn again and again... just so you could stitch them back... and I can see holes... ripped edges... and parched ends... and I don't know if I'll ever be able to stitch them for good... in such a way that it will never be ripped off again... but I know... I'll try my best... and I'll try at it every single minute... every single hour... every single day... and I'll never get tired of it... but I'll do it... only on your terms... the way you want it to be done..."

She listened and listened and listened... and from the corner of her eyes... rolled down few heavy tear drops... that were threatening to roll down... and she knew... she wasn't sad... her tears were not of sadness... but of relief that she'd finally found a home where she belonged... of happiness that she's finally being loved the way she wanted to be loved and cherished... of gratitude to the gods she believed that finally she's come where she was meant to come after all those troubles that she's been through... and the gratitude she felt was at such peak level that she wouldn't complain even if she died right then and there... for she would be happily going to the afterlife... but then again... she couldn't leave him... so she ran her fingers through his hair... again and again... just as it's... and he could feel... from the silence... from the touch of her fingertips... that after so much of broken years in her life... she was finally happy... and she was finally finding courage to let go and move on... to whatever future they've dreamt of... together...

***

XI

Conversation Eleven...

She was sitting on a chair in front of a table that was against a window... as he came to the room... the view showing a lot of trees with thick trunks and generous umbrella of branches and leaves... She was still staring out of the window at the two squirrels running around and he hoped that he hadn't interrupted her... He stood there silently leaning against the wall with his arms crossed... watching her...

"Do you think we're better because we've evolved brains...?" She asked out of the blue and he realised that his presence didn't go unnoticed...

"We can communicate better because we've evolved brains..." He replied... still leaning against the wall...

She jerked and turned to look at him leaning against the wall... and smiling at her...

"Do you think we're better because we've evolved brains...?" She repeated her question and he realised that she wasn't at all satisfied with whatever answer he'd given her... He smiled widely at the thought...

"No... I don't think so..."

"Why do you think we're not better than the animals...?"

"I don't have an answer to it... actually... I can only tell you my viewpoint..."

"I'd like that..."

He unfolded his hands and walked towards her... He grabbed a chair from the corner and sat close to her... He let out his hand... palm upwards... and she held his hand... their fingers interlocking...

"I guess it's the greed that dominates us all... and the rest of it... are just its minions..."

She looked at him with an eye brow raised... It's the first time she's heard this kind of a view... He smiled once again and continued...

"Some people are greedy for wealth... some for luxury... some for intimacy... some for upholding their status... and so many other reasons that are personal to each... unique to each... In an effort to satisfy their greed... they would bring about the minions like ego, toxicity, ignorance, jealousy, stealing, cheating, murder and so on... Some minions are bigger than other minions... That's all... And those who dream of the bare minimum get trapped in the crossfire..."

"Why do they get trapped in the crossfire...?"

"They trust that the world is better than what it actually is... or at least they trust..." He trailed off in his thoughts and he began rubbing her hand with his thumb quite subconsciously... "... they trust that the world could do better than this... a fool's hope..."

She leaned towards him and held at the side of his neck and kissed him on his forehead... He looked at her eyes and he could see that he wasn't the only fool in this world...

She was there too... with him... He held at the side of her neck and they bumped their forehead gently and stayed just like that... their foreheads communicating what the whole world couldn't...

***

XII

Conversation Twelve...

She kept staring at him as he came out of the bathroom and dressed himself... It wasn't a sort of a stare that was born out of lust... but she was just watching... so casually... and he kept watching her too... smiling...

"I can see something is bothering you..." He said looking at her as he buttoned up his pants...

"I'm luckier than I thought I was..." She whispered loud enough for him to hear... "... you're with me..."

She had told him this a million times... but this time... it seemed quite different... "... I'm much luckier than you... to have you..." He said... searching her eyes for more... He felt... there's something lingering behind...

"I'm luckier to see red flags when they come... I'm luckier to escape those red flags when they come..."

"Am I a red flag to you...?"

She was startled at the question and looked at him... her gaze focused at his eyes... "What...! No... No... you're not a red flag... I wasn't talking about you..."

He knew it... he knew it wasn't him she was talking about... But he wanted to be sure... he wanted to know how she saw him... how he'd made her feel... And he knew... she was about to talk about someone in her past... He dried his hair with his towel and went and sat near her... He smelled of butterfly pea...

"Can I hold your hand...?"

"Yes..." She said... her eyes lingering on his fingers interlocking with hers... "I was talking about the rest... those people... them..."

He knew... he knew well... But he wanted her to open up... She looked at his eyes quite unexpectedly and held her gaze there...

"I've been through too much of toxic relationships... I thought... I thought I'd never be able to be stable in a relationship... love someone once again... give 100% to that person... and I'm lucky that person is you... and I feel equally satisfied... because... because..." Her thoughts trailed off and he waited patiently... looking at her eyes... "... because you give me 100% too... and that's... that's... new... and relieving... I... I... feel so lucky..."

He smiled... his eyes filling up gradually... "Can I kiss you on your forehead...?"

"Yes..."

He leaned towards her forehead and kissed her there... his lips making a lasting impression on her forehead...

"I'll always be like that to you... I don't know how to love you otherwise..."

Her eyes filled up gradually too... She threw her arms around his neck and hugged him close... the butterfly pea scent growing stronger as she went closer to him... little water drops dripping down to the back of her neck from his hair... He pressed his lips fiercely on her neck... and his hands tighter around her ribs...

"I won't leave you... I'll always love you... even if it destroys me..." He whispered to her neck...

"And I'll always love you too..." She whispered back to his skin...

***

XIII

Conversation Thirteen...

She hugged *The Great Gatsby* to her chest and lied staring at the ceiling... The night had already grown darker and there was some long-lost expression lingering behind... For her... it seemed like Gatsby had still remained in the room where she'd completed the book...

"Have you felt the presence of characters long after you've completed the book...?" She asked out of the blue... and he raised his head all of a sudden from *Pride and Prejudice*... He too was almost at the end...

"...?"

"You know..." There was a huge pause... Her eyes just drifted off into some space behind him and he could feel that she was seeing someone else there... someone he definitely couldn't see...

"... you know... the Weasley twins... Snape... Sam... Rowan... Plath... and now Gatsby... too many people still linger behind... at least their ghosts... and they keep me company... not completely leaving me... you know..."

He knew... Even though he's familiar with her having the blurred boundary... but not familiar with... personally... he knew... he knew all of it...

"Do you want them to leave...?"

She looked at him as if he'd sinned... but then her expression softened and she sighed... "I don't know... eventually they might harm me... but now... I'd like to have them..."

"Why do you think they might harm you...?"

"Normal society doesn't entertain abnormal people like me... do they...?"

"No... but you're not alone..."

She knew what he meant in that very instant... She could see it in his eyes...

"I know..."

And he knew what she meant too... in her words... from her eyes...

***

XIV
Conversation Fourteen...

He sat with *The Fault in our Stars* on the beanbag... his eyes focused on each and every word... She kept watching him read... He looked at her as he felt her presence...

"How can you read that book again...? Haven't you read it already...?"

"I feel it normal... Can't you read a book that you've read once... again...?"

"No... I already know every detail... and reading it is like... watching a movie whose spoilers you already know..."

"Hmm..." There was a huge pause and his fingers traced over the cover of the book as if he was trying to feel the story... "... for me... it's always new... it's always brand new..."

"You're lucky... I never could do that..."

"Would you feel the same about our love too...?" He asked out of the blue...

"Where did that come from...?"

"Come on... tell me..."

"No…"

"Why…?"

"I don't know… Maybe it's because… every single time… it's kinda new…" There was another huge pause… and she was thinking of the right words… "… this is how you feel about books…!!!" She told it more to herself than to him…

"Indeed…"

"Maybe I was waiting for the right book after all…?"

"Me…?"

"Yeah… you're not simply a novel… you're a poetry collection… of different genres… different moods… different styles… I would never grow tired of you…"

"Hmm… How would you want to recite my poems then…?"

She smiled in a mischievous manner and went towards him… She smiled playfully… and took the book from his hand… remembered to keep the bookmark and placed it on the table… and sat in his lap with her legs apart… and facing him straight…

"I would write you with my fingertips… and I would recite you with my lips…"

Saying this… she leaned in and kissed his forehead… then she smiled quite playfully and kissed his mouth… their lips interlocking… and their fingertips writing poetry…

***

XV

Conversation Fifteen...

"Plath...?"

"Mmm...?"

"What's something that you regret the most...?"

"Growing up..."

"Why...?"

Plath looked at him in disbelief as if assuming the fact that any baby could understand what she meant by that... slamming her book closed. She was currently on *Lapvona*. It was lent to her by someone she knew.

"When you grow up..." she said running her fingers along the hard bound edges as if she was feeling the intensity of the fiction. "... you come into terms with your permanency of unhappiness... You smile and laugh at occasion... but none of it ever see the sunlight through your eyes... You just pretend and pretend until you cannot distinguish it from your own skin... the way a mask sticks into your own very skin. When you were a babe... you were happy... and every single person could see it in your eyes... But now... every single person can see grief in yours... even if you smile... even when you laugh..."

Freud was lost in analysis of what she had just said. He kept staring at the way she subconsciously ran her fingers through the edge of the hard bound book... The lamb on its thick black cover seemed to be moving along with her fingers... dancing to the words she had said... as if agreeing to it.

"What do you think about me then...? Am I happy... or am I pretentious of my happiness...?" he asked looking at her eyes... tearing his gaze from her fingers...

"Everyone is pretentious of their happiness..." she said looking back into his eyes... "... even you... most times... That's how we grow up... I don't think we can change that part of growing up..." There was a short pause as if she was trying to find the right words. "Nevertheless... I believe I've changed your permanent unhappiness in a better way... I believe I've given you reason enough to look forward with hope... to laugh forgetting the unhappiness that strikes so often... to smile even when the whole hell breaks loose... just the way you've done for me..."

Again, there was a pause... this time... it was his turn to find the right words... He knew Plath was always this person who would tell the truth no matter how brutal it seemed and felt... But this time... she seemed to have said it beautifully and precisely... more like Dante's Beatrice.

"You've..." was all that he could tell and he felt embarrassed by the way he had said it... He stretched out his hand to squeeze her feet that was stretched out to his lap from her beanbag to his as if to tell her everything that his limited vocabulary couldn't... and like every time... she smiled at his warm gesture...

MAALU...

***

XVI

Conversation Sixteen...

He was throwing a lavender cricket ball up and catching it for the simple feel of its designs against his palms... She watched him throw the ball... and rarely... few of the throws actually hitting the ceiling and creating tiny incomplete splotches of smudged black circles... It seemed as if he was controlling whether the ball should hit or not... the feeling... the dream he had come to forget... or at least... pretended to forget before everyone else's eyes...

She admired that about him... him never letting go of his dream just like that... It also made her sad too... if they had little bit of time and money... she would have volunteered to help him get into the best academy and would do what needs to be done... She knew she could've thrown him into the best school for cricket as if he was a kitten in a bag despite all his protests of missing her too much... or not being able to see her... he would somehow have made it there... and somehow become happier... She knew it wasn't her fault that he couldn't actually chase down his dream but the popular thought of the society that kids could get nowhere with sports... a pandemic that had hit his parents too...

"Are you happy...?" she asked out of the blue even when she knew what he was going to answer back...

"Yes..." he replied automatically... still throwing the ball to the ceiling... "Why do you ask...?"

"You couldn't follow your dream..."

He caught the ball with his left hand which definitely wasn't his strong hand and stared at it for a while trying to bring it back to life... trying to go back to his childhood and blow back life into it... like many a times he did with his cricket bat... like many a times he did with his field keeping... like many a times he did with his wicket keeping...

"I did fulfil my dream..." he said staring at the ball refusing to take his eyes off... as if it might vanish if he did...

"What dream of yours have you fulfilled...?"

"I have you..."

"I'm not your dream..."

"No... You're not my dream..." he said... finally peeling his eyes off of the ball in his hand... but his fingers tightening its grip around it... "... Being with you is my dream... being part of you... losing myself in you... and diving deep down to find me again... The whole endless search for myself... even though I know I'm there in you... and you're there in me... a search that's eternal... but somehow beautiful in its own way... That's my dream..."

"What about the one in your hand...?"

"Oh...?" He looked into his hands as if he was suddenly aware of the ball's presence... the hard rubbery texture... the scent of his childhood mixed with the scent of dust and sweat and leather and vivid coloured jerseys... "... This...?"

There was a long pause as if he was fumbling through a mixture of words and thoughts and memories... "... Not all dreams come true... do they...?"

Her face fell... They definitely weren't in a utopian society after all... Sacrifice wasn't a term they were unfamiliar with... They'd learnt it from a very young age onwards... when their mothers yelled at them... how much they'd sacrificed for them... when their fathers had yelled at them... how much sweat they'd spent on them... when even being born wasn't their choice... the sacrifice that was thrust upon them by birth...

"But I'm glad..." he said breaking her reverie... "I'm glad it's not you whom I lost... I could live with... losing this..." he said looking longingly at the ball in his hand... "... but I don't think I can survive losing you..."

"What if..." her voice broke as she asked it... "... what if you never met me... and you'd that dream...? That would've been better... wouldn't it...?"

"If I hadn't met you...? Mmm... I don't know about that thought... But I know one thing..." he said staring at her eyes... the grip on the ball losing a bit... "... before I met you... I was a living hell... living... breathing... walking hell... You showed me that I was not entirely... you know... unlovable... You showed me... that I'm worthy of that love... that I'm worthy of *your* love... That's huge..."

"But what about that...?" she asked looking at the ball feeling sorry and... in some way... guilty... assuming it's because he met her that he'd lost his dream...

"What about it...! At least I got someone with whom I could play it with..." he said throwing it right at her... and she... out of the reflexes she'd got from her childhood cricket games... which wasn't much... she caught it smoothly... mainly because the throw was quite easy...

"So... you're not mad at me...?"

"Why should I...? It seems I'm the luckiest... to have ever meet you... and have you with me... and to cherish your presence... and to love... and this harmony we have... this connection... everything... I couldn't ask for more..."

She threw the ball back... smiling at him... and he caught the ball smoothly...

"Do you want to play in our bedroom...? It's getting late anyway..." he said tossing over the ball at her... she caught the ball as she blushed deep red like a tomato... She threw the ball hardly just below his knee...

"Ouch... that wasn't very nice..." he squealed in pain...

"At least... I got a smooth LBW..." she winked... and he laughed rubbing his leg...

***

XVII
Conversation Seventeen...

"How would you like to die... if you could actually choose...?" she asked staring at his eyes...

"What...?"

"You know... like a choice... if you had one that is..."

"You tell me first then..."

"I would... in normal case of course... picture my death as less dark than I usually picture... You know... like I would probably be sitting by the window in a car... you'll be driving probably... I'll be looking out through the window... our music system blasting with songs we love... and I would be lost in thoughts... thinking how bright the day is... but eventually... my vision fades... and it becomes black... and death takes me... while you're with me... silently and peacefully... I won't be afraid... you'll be with me..."

"What would I do then... if you're gone...?"

"You tell me... how you would like to die..."

"If that's how you die... I'd park the car on the side of the road... and then... I would lie down on your lap... my tears would wet your clothes... I know... I could almost picture it... but if my vision fades just like that... and if I die then and there too... I'd be happier than you think... to come up with you... along with you..."

"That would be beautiful..."

He smiled at what she said... At least... both of them had a clear idea on how to die together... whether that wish would be granted or not... will be an entirely different matter...

***

XVIII
Conversation Eighteen...

"Do you know what I like about our meetings...?" she asked holding on his little finger with her little finger...

"Tell me..."

"None of our meetings are pre-planned... I didn't plan to meet you... All I had was a fantasy of meeting a person whose standards I've kept so high I was so sure no one... literally no one is going to reach there... I was positive on that fact..."

"Really...?" he asked smiling and turning towards her... facing her... his hand gently resting on her cheek... their little bed creaking under his weight...

"Yeah... I mean... I knew I was a fantasy person... and I believed that my fantasy would lead me to have fantasies about my life as well... and in general... these concepts seemed a fantasy too... not reality... and I thought... I'd either end up alone or I'd have to force myself to love someone whom I cannot love in the first place... I don't know where you come from... but I know if you go... I'd come with you too... wherever that maybe...”

“You seem unusually chatty tonight... What happened...? Are you happy...?”

“I'm always happy when I'm with you... You put my mind in peace... I don't know how you do it... I don't know if I ever want to know it... But I hope it stays that way always...”

He held on tight to her pinky finger and kissed it... “All I need is this assurance... all I need is you... This trust that you'll stay with me always... this miracle that you've transformed my life into... I need only you... everything about you...”

“You brought divinity into my life... not just a miracle... and I hope I'd be able to cherish this until the day I die... and even long after that... lives after lives... That would be my dream...”

“I thought your dream was to be a writer...”

She mock-frowned at him and pinched him on his upper arm... “Ouch...” he squealed... “... you do pinch me a lot...”

“I've more than one dream... and indeed... my writings do make you immortal... You'll live in me... through my words... my sentences... my thoughts... my memories and dreams...”

“I never asked for that... I just wanted someone to finally understand me... a great riddle everyone pretended I'm...”

“You're indeed a riddle... no doubt on that... But you're a riddle that I understand... and that which I can solve... I guess I'm just like that to you too...”

“I'll always understand you... Always...”

“And I'll understand you always too...”

***

XIX

Conversation Nineteen...

"People tend to forget to mention the ones that had died in their family... don't they...? Especially the ones who killed themselves when they were still young and appeared to be healthy...?" she asked one night all of a sudden... her fingers entangling on the hem of her T-shirt...

"Whom do you have in mind...?" he asked staring at her posture that indirectly told him that she was tired... not physically... but mentally... emotionally...

"Tell me... the answer... Why... why do they tend to forget them...?"

"I'm not an expert to get you the right answer... but I'll try my best to tell you my opinion... Is that fine with you...?"

"Yes... I would love that..."

"I think... I think that they desperately try to forget their death more than their existence because... at least for some... they have this guilt that it's because of them that their loved ones killed themselves... it's because of them not being there for that person that they killed themselves... It's like a loop... where the thoughts come on and on... repeatedly like a broken record... even when they know from deep within that they've done their best... heard their best... listened their best... and still they've this guilt haunting them... that they could've done better still..." There was a pause as if he was trying to think things through... "... because they're not trying to forget the dead person... they're trying to forget the pain... but pain doesn't work that way... does it...? Because pain demands to be felt... That's what Gus told... right...?"

She knew that his memory was spot on... but she never thought that he'd quote from the first book she gave him to read... the very first book that connected them...

"I guess..." she replied looking at his eyes... seemingly lost in him... "... does memory really hurt...?"

"How did you feel when he died...?"

She knew whom he was mentioning... She hasn't seen his body... she hasn't seen much... But she knew... how he died... and how his death had affected the family... She took a deep breath and looked into his eyes...

"I didn't cry... not even at night... I told myself... I'd kids to answer to... to look after... I couldn't feel that pain... I wanted to feel it... cry it out... but I couldn't... Still... I haven't accepted his death... I think it's because I didn't see his dead body... I didn't even see his death... I don't ever want to see anybody's death... but... maybe if I'd seen something... I could get closure... you know..."

He hugged her close and kissed on her forehead... "I know... I know..."

***

XX
Conversation Twenty...

He could see a dark silhouette on the canvas of the moonlit window... He knew who it was and he knew by her posture... her posture of sitting up with her knees hugged closer to her chest... that she wasn't in a very good mood... He wanted to know what the time was but switching on the light nor taking his phone from the bedside table would help him now... She didn't want light to disturb her dark melancholy... He rubbed gently over her backbone and he could feel her relax at his touch...

"What's it... that's bothering you tonight...?" he wasn't really surprised of her insomnia... In fact... she had warned him of her mood swings and insomnia and how hard it would be for him to adjust to her lifestyle... that she was more of a loner type rather than a family woman... But he loved her despite all of that... It was never a lack in his eyes... and it was never too much either... It was just the right amount... and he understood it somehow...

"In my old home..." she began... trying her best to give him a mental image of the house... "... in front... there was this long cream coloured sofa which wasn't cream before... Most of the furniture in that house is much older than I'm... rusted and worn off... In the beginning... it was just... you know... a red sofa with all those rust... that accompanied with advices of not to be too hard on the age-old sofa..." she paused... Her posture didn't change even when she said those words... He wanted to get up and sit side by side with her... but he wanted her to have her privacy too... If she wanted him side by side... she would've woken him up from his sleep... which was also very familiar to him... She had no such formalities... and for some reason... he liked it too... He knew she wouldn't just vanish... he needn't worry about her vanishing...

"... I lied on it at night once... because I didn't want to lie down and hurt my back... so I lied on the widest sofa I could get... but I couldn't sleep..." she paused again as if she was watching it in pictures right before her eyes... on the darkened wall... "... My uncle used to lie there... on the sofa... at nights... And that night... I couldn't sleep... My heart started beating so fast... as if my body was building up adrenaline for flight... I literally started sweating and panicking... It seems strange to you... but I wasn't getting afraid of the night or the dogs barking in the distant... I was getting afraid of the voice that called me... My uncle... he kept calling me in the middle of the night... and my brain took on the logic side... telling me that's not possible... because... you know... he's dead... and I've told you..."

Yes... She'd told him... Her uncle had hanged himself from the ceiling fan in the upstairs room... It was hard for her to go upstairs from that incident onwards... but she never showed... The people around could barely understand it...

"... He... he called me in the middle of the night... definitely after 12... and he kept urging me to go with him upstairs... to that room... you know..." He knew... "... asking me to fetch a bedsheet on the way... long enough for me to... you know..."

"Weren't you... how did you manage to... I mean... all alone... I wasn't there... I..."

"I know... and that scared me more... I tried calling as many Gods as I can... but it didn't work... It was as if I was shouting into the void... you know..." There was another great pause as if she was rummaging up her brains for the right words... "... They... they act as if they've forgotten... or that it doesn't bother them anymore... or pretend that such a person never existed in our family... as if talking about him would blow up the whole family into smithereens... It's like... it's like I'm living inside this time bomb that would blow up one day... and one day... it would blow me up along with it..."

He didn't take his hand from behind her... neither did he get up and sit side by side with her...

"I would be sad if you go..." he said...

"I know... that's the only anchor that stood me in place... or else... I don't know what I would've done... You know... I can't control how my body moves and does when I'm numb... It's like my limbs act in its own way... like they've their own manual how to work... you know... I wish I could control... like I've been doing all these years... I hope your smiling face acts as my anchor every single time... I hope... I hope..."

He rubbed behind her... gently but strongly... trying to let her know that he was with her no matter what... and as in response... she leaned towards his touch... It was a miracle how they could communicate without words at desperate times... These wordless communications relieved her so much... he knew... she'd told him... She needn't explain every single thing every single time... she needn't try hard in this relationship... For the first time in a relationship... she was herself... and it wasn't a terror...

"Would you like to cuddle in my chest...?" he asked gently...

"I would love that..." her voice trembled and he knew she was trying to hold back her tears... He stretched his arms wide enough for her to cuddle... an invitation she took gladly... and lied down gently... They intertwined their pinky fingers and he held on tighter...

"Whenever you get scared of those shadows you see... or the voices you hear... just hold onto my pinky finger like this... You're never alone... and you'll never be alone... I'll always be with you..."

"Thank you for being there for me... I love you..."

"I love you more..."

***

XXI

Conversation Twenty One...

"Does sincerity and passion for one's work really matter... especially... in the teaching field...?" she asked out of the blue... her eyes fixated on the words in the book she was reading... She was comfortably cuddled on her beanbag with a thick blanket draped around her feet... She was the kind of person who couldn't tolerate even a little bit of cold...

"Why do you ask...?"

"I don't think anyone wants a sincere teacher... especially the authorities... I mean... the kids dig it... but the authorities... I don't think they really do need them..."

"Why do you think so...?"

"Because sincere teachers... they force the lazy ones to work... you know... like go an extra mile for the better results... But the lazy ones... they're used to their lazy routine... They don't want to work the extra mile... they just want to sit idly and loot some money that they claim is their salary... What do the kids get...? I mean... they pay the fee... they show up to their class... they're forced to sit inside their classrooms which are nothing but four walls... and repeat whatever the hell their teachers teach them... no matter what..."

"Do you feel bad for the kids...?"

"I do... I really... really do... I mean... I was a student... and I hated the way the money was spent to feed lazy teachers for no apparent reason... I mean... they never improved us... But I've seen rare ones too... you know... the ones who did actually made me better... turned me into a better version of myself... teachers who gave me fire... in some way like Prometheus I guess..." Her face lit up as she spoke of it...

"Nowadays no one wants sincerity... I guess... They don't want fun teachers who can enlighten them up... nor open up their mind to new thoughts and creativity... They just want grades and it's the end of it..."

"I feel sorry for the kids... you know... they could've reached great heights if they'd better teachers... those who can actually... you know... guide them... open them up... ask them to think their ways... you know..."

"I know..."

"I don't think somebody can prevent mischief by completely denying their right to explore... their right to curiosity... The more you deny... the more curious they'd get... They should've been taught everything and how to handle it all with responsibility... they shouldn't be denied their mistakes of their age... but should've been taught how to learn from it..."

"No one wants that now... No one... It's just how the world is..."

"I guess the world would suffer for it then... greatly... actually... They'll be creating generations of zombies then..."

"I guess..."
"I hate what the world has turned into..."
"I hate it too..."

***

XXII
Conversation Twenty Two...

"I always felt that you bite more than you can chew... you know... in terms of sufferings in life..." he said pouring a glass of grape wine for both of them... He also threw in two ice cubes each...

"Bring the bottle..." she said casually trying to avoid the question... He brought the bottle as well which was kind of tricky for him and laid them out on the coffee table... He then sat next to her on his beanbag... He handed over one glass to her and stared at her eyes...

"Are you okay...?" he asked taking a sip from his glass...

"Yes..." she said abruptly... "... What made you think I wasn't...?"

"I didn't get an answer..."

"I... I don't know what to say... about the "you bite more than you can chew" part... Maybe... maybe not... I don't know..."

His eyes flickered over to her scars on her wrist and then back to her eyes... His eyes seemed to him... was proving a point...

"What do you want me to say...?" she asked noticing his gaze... She sipped her wine and looked into the violet droplets of the wine on the brim of the glass... "I don't know if it's too much for me or not... I've endured it... and most of the part... I'd no one to help me... I'm aware of that much... Besides I don't think God would give us more to bite than we can chew... right...?" There was a pause as if she was pondering over that thought... "... Maybe its me... maybe I'm weak..."

"No..." he protested all of a sudden that he created little waves of protest in his wine glass as well... The droplets escaped out of their prison and splashed onto his pants... creating an aesthetic splotch... "... I totally disagree that..." he said rubbing on his pants knowing clearly that he's only making it worse... "... You're not weak... On the contrary... I think you're more powerful than you think... You... you didn't give up..." he said... his eyes still wandering over to her scars...

"Powerful..." she repeated with a tinge of contempt lingering at the tip of her tongue... "... I'm tired of being powerful and strong and pushing forward... Most of the time I've wished if I could just end it... you know... just give up... and sleep... and never wake up... But life doesn't work that way... does it...! We wake up and wake up and wake up until it's our time... the whole routine repeating like a cycle... I wish this loop would be over..."

"Do... do you still feel the same... to end it...?"

She began swirling her glass creating tiny whirlpool inside... taking care not to spill it... The ice cubes were indeed creating chaos with the whirlpool... "It's not about you... at least this isn't... It's not about us either... It's just me... me and my broken brain..."

"What should I do...?"

"I don't know... I don't even know if there's a permanent cure for this... or at least a temporary one... I just know that it's haunting me and at times it's scary..."

"Can I hold your pinky finger...?"

"Yes..."

"You know... you know me... I never do anything without asking you..." he said... holding her pinky finger with his...

"Do you still feel the same when I hold you...?"

"At times... but when you hold me... it's bearable... At least I know... that I'm not alone..."

He kissed on her pinky finger and smiled at her...

"At least... we're sane enough for wine..." she said with a wink...

"That we're..."

And they laughed softly... and loved gently into the night...

***

XXIII

Conversation Twenty Three...

She stared into the sparkly ring on her finger that he had so lovingly put on her finger... It wasn't an engagement ring with a flashy diamond... but it was something they found online... a couple ring made of silver where her ring had a shape of a pointed crown while his ring was more like a caved in band of silver... She loved staring at the ring when she felt lost and hopeless... it gave her a sense of coming back home to him...

"Does it ever hurt you... when people don't appreciate you no matter how much you put yourself out there... like you know... them asking more and more from you...?"

He looked at her fingers... the ring he'd put on her finger... It was a beautiful day... He had never seen her that happy before... the way she'd looked at her finger... the way she'd looked at him and kissed him... It didn't matter to them if it was made of a real diamond or fake stones... What mattered to them was the gesture... the love... the excitement... and above all... the trust and the commitment... It took them to a whole new world...

"That's how the world is... I suppose..." he said... looking at her face... She raised her gaze towards his eyes and frowned as if he'd said the wrong answer...

"I do know that..." she said and paused gently at the ending... letting it hang onto the tip of her tongue... his brain trying to process what kind of a pause that was... "I wanted to know if that ever hurt you..."

"It did... it hurt me a great deal... it still does... It does make me hopeless most of the time... but that's what today's world is about... No one wants the effort you put... or the time you spend for all the information you conjure up just so you can enlighten that person too... not to boost up your ego or anything... but for the pure pleasure of... you know... enlightening them... you know what I mean...?"

"I do..." she paused again staring at his eyes... Out of all the people around him... she knew exactly... what he meant by those words... "When I was younger... I used to think about going around the whole world... finding people who genuinely loved learning... especially literature... and other arts... forming a little club of their own... probably giving them a fun name like *Pastel Potatoes*... I don't know why that name came onto my mind... but it came... anyway... forming the club... engaging fun conversations at midnight... probably in a huge room under the sky with lots of beds... you know... just in case if they fell asleep... and talking things over... you know...?"

"Whoa...! I never thought you had thought about all these..." he said... and she blushed at the thought...

"I did... I wanted to discuss about poetry... and novels... and every individual perspective that I could conjure up... you know... And some funny arguments... and stuff like that... you know... But I rarely found people like that..."

"I know..." he said and looked apologetically at her... "But... can I tell you my honest opinion...?"

"Yes..."

"You rarely found those people because you were in the wrong circle... you know... you've been stuck with people who gossip and tell bad behind you... I guess you need to change your circle..."

"Well... then I guess you'll have too... You need a circle of people who are genuinely interested in cricket... you know...?"

"Is it too hard to find someone who's a writer and a cricket freak.... all in one...?"

"I don't know... you tell me..."

"Well..." he said... pretending to be thinking too hardly for it... "... I guess... it was hard at first... but I believe... I've found a person just like that..."

"Really...?"

"For real... you make me the luckiest person in this whole world..."

"I guess it works both ways..."

They held each other's hands and gently gave a squeeze...

***

XXIV
Conversation Twenty Four...

He was preparing sandwiches for both of them in the kitchen... He made sure she got more cucumbers and tomatoes as she loved them so dearly... He took the sandwiches in a large plate and poured two glasses of grape wine and marched off to the living room where she was reading... as he assumed... But quite contrary to his assumption... she was sketching something on the back pages of her notebook...

He gently kept the plate on the coffee table and joined beside her on the beanbag... She stared at him as he looked over her shoulder to know what she was sketching out...

"The Shadows..." she whispered without waiting for his question... "I've started seeing them again... They are all over my dreams when I sleep... and even in our room... by the corner... when I wake up in the middle of the night... They're just staring... you know... with huge red eyes... and lean... long arms... and claws..."

"Shadows...?"

"Yeah... Shadows..."

He was totally at a loss... He wanted to ask a million little questions... If this was metaphorical or real... If it was indeed metaphorical... what was it a metaphor of... Was she okay... If he could help her in any way... Should he guard her sleep by staying awake... Or if he should wait until she slept... If he should cuddle her tight so she could sleep better... and many more such questions just popped up in his brain... He watched as the little droplets of condensed vapour stuck onto the glass... running down... racing other droplets... which he assumed was a common nostalgia of every single child who appreciated rain...

"They're metaphorical..." she replied as if she'd read his mind... "I guess... more like a projection of my unhealthy mind..."

"Are you scared...?"

She gulped as she looked at him... She needn't say... It seemed that reading minds worked both ways...

"What can I do for you...?" he asked...

"I don't know... I'm afraid... Maybe not knowing is what scares me... you know... I don't know myself... what to do... to save me... I just know that I feel safe with you now... I don't even know if I'll stop feeling safe or anything... It's like... I've no guarantee over myself... That scares me..."

"Does it mean... you would leave me...?"

"I don't know... I know I don't want to... I... they... they're scary... these Shadows... I don't know what to do..."

"Hmm..." There was a great pause... His brain kept searching for a possible solution... "Can you do me a favour then...?" he asked as if he reached the conclusion...

"Tell me..."

"Can you hold my pinky finger with yours when you get scared...? I know I've asked this a million times... but... you know... I don't care when it's... you know... late at night... or if I'm sleeping... or if I'm doing something important... Just come to me... let me know... and hold my pinky finger... okay...?"

"Okay..."

"Maybe Okay will be our Always... as Gus put it..."

She giggled softly hugging him close to her... It was a moment she would cherish... she knew it... something that told her that he's there for her no matter what...

***

XXV

Conversation Twenty Five...

She drank a glass of last night's grape wine in a go and refilled herself... It was like she was desperate to get drunk even when knowing that the wine he made were definitely not alcoholic... She kept drinking it over and over again...

"What is it that you're doing...?" he asked raising his gaze from the book he was reading... and looking over to her worried sick...

"I'm trying to get drunk... What do you think I'm doing...?"

"With a non-alcoholic wine...?"

"I don't need alcohol to get high... I just need to trick my brain and that's enough..."

"Why do you want to get drunk...?" he asked... his voice genuinely getting tensed and edgy...

"Because I'm tired of pretending that I'm happy... I'm tired of looking cheerful and happy and all those colourful appearances with short hair and makeup... I thought I'd feel like myself more after getting a short hair... but it seems like I don't know myself quite well... I've been pretending my whole life to be somebody else... to please the rest... I forgot who I'm or what I'm..."

"What happened...?"

"You know... sometimes I watch people talk and say all kinds of nonsense... the terrible gossip that we both so hate... but they seem more happier than us... They just go around speaking ill of others and they end up being this lucky... happy people... who get to have everything they need... and our hard work... it just would pay off to nothing no matter what..."

"Hey... hey... hey..." he said now genuinely concerned and getting up from his beanbag and walking over to her... His copy of *Norwegian Wood* neatly kept on the coffee table with a bookmark in between... "Is it okay if I hug you...?"

She nodded silently... her eyes bloodshot that he almost feared that her way of tricking her brain was spot on... "Can you hold my pinky finger...?" he asked kissing above her head... She held onto his pinky finger with her own and he smiled into her hair... Her hair smelled of neem and hibiscus... "Now tell me... what's bothering you at this time of the night...?"

"You might think I'm stupid..."

"Hey... I'm interrupting you right there... Have I ever told you that...?"

"No..."

"So... don't you ever think like that again... Okay...? Now... continue..."

She snuggled into his chest and took a deep breath... He smelled of jasmine and something unique that was him...

"I look at random people sometimes... mostly when I'm waiting for a bus... or when I'm in a bakery... having an ice cream... The people around... they look so happy and perfect... and I think... why can't I be happy..." she paused as if she was thinking about what she really wanted to stress about... "... I know that they are not completely happy and stuff like that... but when I look at them... I wonder... I finally get the guy I've always wanted... this amazing wonderful human being who's not like the rest of the guys... who actually literally asks me consent for everything he does... whose heart strings my heart has connected with... but..." she paused again and now... he could feel fresh hot tears drenching his T-shirt... "... sometimes I think I'm cursed... you know... never to feel happy ever... despite all the wonderfulness that has happened to me... I keep thinking that some day... I'll end up being a burden to you too... making you hate me for who I'm... what I'm... my sickness that has been passed onto me by genes... which I'd no control or so ever... you know... It's not like I asked to be born or anything..."

"I know..." he said hugging her closer to his chest... she could literally hear his heart beat if she really concentrated... and for some time... his heart beating against her ear drum calmed her... "... I knew this about you from the day we began talking... I knew I wasn't going get anything normal with you... and I'm not complaining... I'm just saying... I'm not normal either... What the society had told everyone as 'normal' has become so outdated and this ideology about normalcy has become so outdated... it marginalises the rest... whom the society pictures as the 'abnormal'... What I really wanted to say was only this... I'm not normal and neither are you... and I know both of us are going to have rough roads up and down our path of hills... but... I think we'll be fine as long as we stick to each other... you know...? I'm not going to say that we'll be perfectly happy... maybe that's not written down in our books by Fate... but we could have tiny moments where we could... you know... forget the taxes... and the gossips... and all the backstabs... and just be in the moment... just you and me... Wouldn't that be perfect... even for a fraction of a second... perfect...?"

"Yes..." she said wiping her eyes with the back of her sleeves... "I guess we'll be perfectly happy just for a fraction of a second..."

"Here's to a million more fractions of seconds..." he said kissing on her head once again... her hibiscus scent filling his lungs...

"Here's to the eternal bliss of fractions of seconds..."

***

XXVI

Conversation Twenty Six...

She was lost in thought as usual but her face showed expressions that resembled grief... He was familiar with her face going blank when she was lost in thought but this grief was painful for him... more than his own at times...

"What is that you are thinking...?" he asked... his fingers knotting the loose thread that he stumbled upon... from where... he doesn't remember...

She looked at him with a blank expression... the grief fading from her eyes and the wrinkles of frustration on her forehead fading into smoothness...

"Nothing..."

"Are you sure...?"

"Yes..."

"I wanted to ask you something... You don't really see me in the list of dreams... do you...?"

She was surprised by that question that he had thrown upon her all of a sudden... She stared at him for a while and then took out her tiny notepad that was resting upon the coffee table and a black pen... He was familiar with her manner of conversation... which transformed into writing when she was about to tell him something serious... She was not confident when it came to speaking... She was more of a writer than a speaker...

She scribbled something seriously on the blank paper and handed it over to him...

No... you're not on that list... But I believe I've told you this before... You're not my dream... at least not anymore... That's why you're not in that list...

"So... you're saying I'm just nobody...?" he asked handing her the notepad back...

No... I didn't say that... I just said that you're not my dream or wish anymore... You used to be a dream... once... I'm not being superstitious here telling you that I dreamt of you even before I met you or anything... but... a guy like you was once my dream... but not anymore... You're a reality... You've become a reality... I've manifested you by demanding my universe that this is the sort of a guy whom I wanted... and here you're... And that's why you're not in that list anymore...

"That is... I don't know what to say... I always thought that you'd be happy without me... that you'd be happy with just your career and success in my life... even if I'm not in it..."

She looked at him with a painful expression that clearly conveyed him that he somehow managed to create a crack in her heart... She scribbled down something hurriedly and handed the notepad back to him...

That's not why I'm obsessing over my career or my success... I thought you understood me... I really thought you did... all these years... You yourself told me that at least one of us needs a job so that we can get married... I was calm until I lost my job... I'm freaking out here because I'm elder to you... and there are pretty good chances for me to get a job first... You've years ahead of you... and I'm stressing myself out and handling my emotions that are clearly like all-hell-loose kind of way... I don't want to scare you with what exactly I'm thinking... If I expose my thoughts without censoring them you would think I'm a psycho... And I don't want... It's the first time in my whole life that I feel I should not lose someone and that if I do... then I'm not just a failure... but a stupid... horrible person too...

He said nothing... He simply stared back at her... It was just that... just that... and she could have just told... but she never did... she never knew how to... The notepad in his palms burnt a hole in his palm as well as in his heart...

***

XXVII

Conversation Twenty Seven...

She was knotting one edge of the scarf that she had worn around her neck as she felt too cold... The way she knotted the scarf was unique... she would tie knots over knots over knots as if she was building a tower out of it... He watched her intently as if she was doing something he had never seen anyone else doing... which was indeed true... he has never seen anyone else do this before... But he had seen her do it a million times before on a piece of rubber band... which snapped because of old age...

"That's beautiful..." he said marvelling the tower she had created out of the knots... She looked at him abruptly as if he had spoken a great folly...

"No... no it's not..." she whispered as if that made enough sense to him... but he couldn't grasp the exact concept she was trying to convey...

"No... it's really beautiful... the tiny knots... and how the colours form a pattern over those knots... It's pretty..." he said encouragingly thinking that this was one of those moments when he told her she was beautiful and she denied it...

She looked at him in the eye sternly this time and pressed on her answer...

"No... it's not pretty..."

"Why's that...?" he asked worrying that somewhere he'd struck a wrong chord...

"These are knots at the end of my scarf of life... building day by day... by the society around me and the culture that it had developed even before I was born..." she began so seriously that he knew he had to pay close attention to it... "... Now... you can see here that the knots build up on the end of the scarf and the scarf is not tied around a chair or a table explicitly restricting me down... preventing me from doing my work or moving around... So... it's easy for me to still move around and do my things and do all that I wish and is capable of... right...?"

"Right..."

"But eventually... over time... this is going to build up a weight as I leave it unnoticed that would... in the future... weigh me down... indirectly preventing me from doing what I love... or even going behind my dreams... Are you following me...?"

"Yes..."

"So... like you said earlier... this does indeed look pretty not because the knots are pretty but because the colours are pretty... which are the colours of this scarf which is a metaphor of my life... The colours of my life are knotted down by invisible forces of authority... tradition and culture... which doesn't seem harmful because ultimately it doesn't directly affect them... but in long term... it does pull you down... killing you slowly and effectively..."

"That's... that's... I don't know... I'm... speechless..."

"I call this *The Illusion of Freedom*..." she said staring at the knots she had created so effectively... and with ease... "... We assume we have all the freedom this 21st century could provide us... but in reality... we're more tied down than our ancestors... and the worse thing is... we consent to it... so it's kind of a long-term effect..."

"Is it possible to untie all these... I mean the knots...?"

She took off the scarf from around her neck and stretched over to his beanbag... "Untie this with me..." she said... and they both began untying the knots... "... Together... I think it's possible... to an extent of course... and I don't just mean man and woman... but the whole world... the whole variety and the uniqueness..."

They untied all the knots quickly and she wore the scarf around her neck once again and leaned back on her beanbag...

"But... this also teaches you one thing... that there's nothing worse in this world than offering to help without them asking for it... And thus... there will always be a fraction of people who still carry their baggage... you know... or maybe jump into their river of chaos and this baggage would drown them down... and there will come times like when... you know... the only thing you can do is just watch and watch... like a helpless audience... and you've nothing to do to help them... because they never asked... and chances are that they're never going to either... And you'll learn one more thing... that it's okay... that... you know... you couldn't save everybody... but you saved somebody... and you saved yourself too... That's what matters by the end of the day... not the count of how many you have saved comparing to the rest who might have saved more people than you... but if you actually saved that one who genuinely asked for it..."

He stared longingly at her eyes and her reassuring smile... blinking at the lack of words his brain was suffering with... and for some reason... all of what she said genuinely made sense... *The Illusion of Freedom...* They were all trapped in it... and he was in it too... along with her... That was all he knew... that some day... they'll swim out of it together... untying all of it together...

***

XXVIII

Conversation Twenty Eight...

It was one of those dark nights when the moon is on the other side of the globe and couldn't make it... She spread herself over the bed as if she was one of the cheese slices in a burger and stared at the ceiling as if somehow that would provide her with some answers...

He was sitting on the desk and writing something down so hurriedly that he wasn't actually paying attention to what she was doing...

"Freud... I was being selfish all this time... haven't I...?"

He stopped writing abruptly and turned towards her... She was still staring at the ceiling without much movement...

"Why do you ask...?" he rested his arm on the backrest of the chair...

"All these years... I've been telling you about my problems and issues... my traumas and trust issues... and everything my mind could remember so as to give you a heads up... I never took your issues into consideration..."

"Oh... that..." he turned towards his paper... his back towards her again... He didn't want to face her... not yet... "... it's nothing really... I mean... comparing to your problems... mine are nothing..."

It was her turn to abruptly turn towards him at his comment... "You cannot compare my problems with yours... no one can do that... Your problems are yours and mine are mine... Doesn't mean that mine is superior to your or that yours is superior to mine..." She stared at the back of his head and he could feel deeply... her gaze piercing his skull...

"I know that... but..."

"I don't think there are much people without mental health issues..." She said staring back to her original spot on the ceiling... "... especially here in this brown nation of brown people... Most of every child's trauma comes from their parents and we've our baggage too... and we'll probably pass it onto the next generation as well until we do something about it..."

"Hmm..." he sunk deeper into his chair wishing if he could suddenly turn invisible... or maybe do something better to fix both of their lives... But that's not how life worked... He can only fix his and she can only fix hers... They can only support each other in the process..."

"Plath...?"

"Hmm...?"

"Do you think we would've had better childhood if we had met earlier...?"

"I don't know... I'm not sure about it... But I guess... we would have been together... through thick and thin... Would that make it better...?"

Yes... yes it would've...

It would've been better...

None of them spoke directly... but both of their hearts did speak... and they knew it...

***

XXIX

Conversation Twenty Nine...

"It's funny when our parents tell us that we should learn from the animals... you know especially when they talk about the independence of their litter..." she ran her fingers along the lines in the book she was writing in... He had given her his ink pen with which she conjured up her muse into the blank pages in front of her... She had just finished and closed the book and stared at him for his answer...

"What do you mean...?"

"You know... when they talk about hens, for example, how they peck on the head of the chicken to stop them from following their mother... or how kittens are left alone when they're old enough to live on their own... It's funny when they say that we should also follow the same... except that we are not taught any of the survival skills that we... as humans... in this society... require..."

"Okay... I understand you... But... what are you getting at...? I think we should indeed learn from the animals... But

I don't get the funny part in it..."

"You know... like... for example... a mother cat teaches its kittens to walk... run around... drink milk from the floor... and to hunt and climb trees... how to escape from predators and potential threats... They teach everything... and then the kittens leave... But in our case... it's not so... you know... I'm not saying we should be taught to climb trees and stuff... but we should be taught some form of martial arts to help us from a threatening situation... or teach us financial management and independence... how to look for jobs... how to not give up no matter how much our life pulls us down... or how to choose our potential partners all by ourselves... by analysing the red flags and green flags... rather than doing it for us... you know... and even sex education... and about consent... and labour division... since women too work nowadays... they're breadwinners too... so the equal division of labour too... you know..."

He knew it well... It was true actually... Humans were the only ones who never teach their young ones to be independent... in every sense... Humans teach their young ones to adjust and suffer the pain... rather than how to survive... He was silent for a long time...

"They think about learning from animals only when their bank balance declines... looking after kids... or getting them married off... Then... they suddenly start worrying about not doing what animals do... That's what's funny about humans... They claim that they're the most evolved species... but they're the most nonsensical so far... What do you think...?"

He could gladly agree with her... He stared at the cover of the book that lied on her lap... staring at the ceiling as if it too had lost its hopes on human life... He nodded absentmindedly as if he was lost in thought... Thinking in detail about it... he too felt it was right... Humans were selfish too... unlike animals... but humans were compassionate too... Humans had both pros and cons... Humans claim that their children are a burden... at least most of them... specifically here... in this brown nation... of brown people.

"Hmm..." He didn't answer right away... It was the kind of conversation that required more and more thought... But he could see the funny part in what she had said... He could identify the hypocrisy that resonated in what they said and what they actually did... Hypocrisy was after all... every human's sibling...

***

XXX

Conversation Thirty...

It was one of those nights again... when she had finished her writing and was quite thrilled to show him what she had written... She... once again looked at the work she had written and called him to read what she'd written...

"Didn't you tell me once that if there was a book written about how people like us should behave in the society... you'd gladly buy it and read it...! Well... it's about that... it's not exactly a book... but more like a short essay... Why don't you read it and give me your thoughts while I make Alu Parathas..."

"Sure... I would love to..." He took the book and looked at the title... but there was none... She hadn't quite decided on one... He smiled and began reading...

"All the world's a stage, and all the men and women merely players..." As Shakespeare once had correctly informed us, living in it also applies to such forms of acting as well. Shakespeare does look like a genius when he informed us of this very

appropriate information, but us, on the other hand, took it a mile further that genuine people do not exist nowadays, but only mimesis of such people exist, and if I remember correctly, Plato had clearly told us that mimesis is the act of imitating that twice removes us from reality. Combining Shakespeare's and Plato's theories together, I come to the assumption that we merely act out in the society as if we are part of The Greatness, but in reality, we are much more fake than the fake-ness that already exists in this world. I write this essay to enlighten people who are innocent and naive, who refuses to be fake and hold out placards of truth over their chests and march over to the world with nothing but those placards made of recycled cardboards and papers and sketch pens. Now, to be really specific, I would like to list out a few major points for people who can identify to this specific category of 'innocent and naive' so as to enlighten them on how to survive this world on their own.

The points of enlightenment are as follows:

1. *Displacement: It is the process of displacing our righteous thoughts with the dominant ideology of the society and nod along like Joseph Tribbiani during conversations. If you take immense care not to voice out your righteous concerns, then you can survive the conversation without being labelled as a 'rebel.'*

2. *Acting without Masks: Now this seems very easy, but it is one of the trickiest for naive people, because naive people tend to express their genuine nature through their gestures even when their lips make contrasting speeches. The best way for this is to smile as best as you can. After all, the expression, 'stabbing in the back with a smile on your face' did not enter the realms of literature for zero reason.*

3. *Observing from the Rear: No, no, no. This is not what you think. This is short for 'observing the person and talking shit*

behind them' kind of mannerisms. (Please ignore the vulgar expressions because most of the naive people like us only understand the profane words. We are, after all, illiterate.) This technique requires a great deal of vocabulary and intellect on how to use them appropriately. It might be hard for naive people to learn this technique, but a good game of scrabbles with your friend or spouse might spice up your brain activity.

4. <u>Acquaintance with Foes</u>: *Now this requires great deal of skills, especially that of creating mental tabular forms. Here, we analyse from 'observing the rear' of the target, who their friends and who their foes are. For this specific talent, we require more details of their foes rather than their friends. But that does not mean we should not find who their friends are. That is an essential part of it too, mainly because we should not talk facts about our target to their friends, but to their foes. That is the most effective way and most assuring method that the news about them will spread like wildfire.*

5. <u>Find your Circle</u>: *Finding your appropriate circle of people who might teach you the basics of these techniques is a must. Despite the fact that I have mentioned this point at the end of the tips and techniques, this remains the most important of them all. Never withdraw into a circle of naive people if you need to learn these techniques. Always learn from the professionals. Observe them closely and imitate them. Absorb their innate talent into you and if you do with utmost dedication, it will soon become a part of you.*

All these points are my personal observations and opinions. This essay might seem incomplete from the society's point of view. After all, I am naive too, even though I do not call myself innocent. The professionals are the ones who genuinely know more about it. This is a summarised version of what I assume are the ways in which one should survive in the society. For more details, it's always better to enquire from the professionals. I hope this essay is comprehensible to you and that this essay may become fruitful in its aim. May your life be fulfilled.

He looked at her from the book as she was boiling the potatoes and heating up the half-cooked chapattis so as to make Alu Parathas.

"You know what...! You should name this essay; *The Ultimate Guide on How to Survive the Society.* It's really sarcastic and I loved it..."

"Really...?" she asked rhetorically. It seemed that she too had her share of giggles as she wrote it.

"Oh yeah..." he answered it even though it's rhetorical. "I think it would be a hit..." She didn't reply to it... She just smiled at him as he joined her in the preparations for their dinner.

***

XXXI

Conversation Thirty One...

She was long lost in her thoughts and he stared at her in such appreciation that any new lover would have toward his loved one... She always got lost in thoughts and it was something he was familiar with. Most of the time... he wanted to just look into her brain and find out what she was thinking or even read her thoughts... but all of those would be prying into her thoughts... without her consent and that would have been something she would not like...

"What are you thinking of...?" he asked... staring into her eyes as if he was bringing them to the real world and anchoring them in place before she would travel into one of her fantasy worlds...

"I dreamt of him... someone I used to love very dearly..."

"Oh..." he whispered... his voice dropping... He had asked her once about this person once and she had told him in detail... and he had also asked her if she would like to leave him one day so that she could be united with him again...

But she'd said no... She'd assured him that... that was not an option she had in mind... and will never have...

"I always had this desperate thought in my mind... more of a wondering... you know... that if I will ever find that right person... But last night... with that dream... I guess I realised... that I had actually found that person..."

"Oh...?" he could say nothing more... His throat just silenced him all of a sudden and crippled him for a brief moment...

"I talked to him as if we were friends... and I told him about you... and I told him why we ended up broken apart... and why I feel much better now with you... I'm not saying I'm special... or as if I'm Mother Teresa... But I always felt like supernatural beings called me... like... if I really listened... I could really hear them... These shadows that called me... might've been part of it... My uncle who called me... might be part of it... And whenever I went to temples... especially of Lord Shiva... I could really feel the vibrations from Him calling me... to join this wonderful place... you know... But I could never go... I always felt that if I went... I would never come back... I had no anchor... no reason to come back... you know... we all have our own duties to our own lives unless we are really called... But with you... I've you to anchor me down... and with you... I feel more connected to Him... more spiritually awakened... but more rooted as well... with enough discipline to keep me in place until I finally reach there... you know..." There was a pause and she sighed deeply... "... I don't know if it makes sense to you... But that's how I feel... Maybe I've gone mad..."

"I... I guess I understand you... Maybe that's your definition of finding the right person..."

"Maybe... I always wanted a person who knew the difference between being religious and being spiritual... you know… the way I see it… religion has a God or multiple Gods in some cases… but spirituality feels energy variations and sees dreams and visions… Religion is nothing but a path… while spirituality is the destination… And… it seems that I always knew that I could never get married to a person who is not spiritual… at least in my terms… you know…?"

"I know…"

"Am I even making sense…?"

"Yes… I guess you're…" he said hugging her close to him… Her dream didn't matter… or whom she saw didn't matter… It was her mind concluding things for her… bringing a closure to her… letting her move on… and it was fine… She wasn't going anywhere… She is coming home actually… She is finally coming home… All her aimless wanderings ended and she was coming home…

***

XXXII

Conversation Thirty Two...

"I used to think always why people who do hard work on field never gets paid as much as the ones who work in front of a computer or the so-called white-collar jobs..." She said when he was least expecting. He was reading *Looking for Alaska* when she abruptly brought the topic in front of him and laid it neatly as if she was unfolding a piece of clothing before the customer...

"What conclusion did you reach...?" He asked staring into something as if he was thinking of something...

"I don't know... I didn't really get a conclusion... But I sure didn't appreciate the conclusion others gave me... I do understand the idea that they get paid less because they don't use their brains like the rest... but that's not even something that we can compare to... I mean... what about their time that they spend... their labour... their sweat... and most of them are too essential that we can barely do anything without them..."

"I see what you're getting at..."

There was a huge silence and both of them simply stared at each other for a long while as if they both had something to convey...

"Can somebody's physical energy and mental energy be compared at all...?"

He didn't have an answer for that... Surely... it was quite impossible for people to actually do that... because... well... physical and mental labour amount to differently... and most of the people who provide physical labour are being exploited...

"It's incomparable..." He agreed in a matter-of-fact voice... There was no answer... he knew... There was no answer that provided justice to everyone at the same time...

"The logic that persists right now doesn't really convince me... you know...?"

"I know..."

This same principle worked years before in families as well... where men were respected well because of their breadwinner qualities while women were neglected or pushed to the corners of a house... He wanted to ask if it hurt her when she was teased for not knowing the household chores when she never liked doing them ever... He wanted to ask if it hurt her when everyone asked her that she should work at her house feeding her future husband and children when she preferred working hard to improve her own skills and her own future... He wanted to ask too many questions but his voice never came out... It betrayed him every single time when he needed it the most...

"If they had a voice... the world would be a lot different from what it's now..."

Times did change... but having a voice doesn't seem like changing any time soon... Is world that hopeless... or is it never going to change...?

***

XXXIII

Conversation Thirty Three...

Everything seemed fine until the book fell from the table and hit the tile with a faint thud... It was as if someone had knocked down the book purposefully from the table... He bent down and picked the book up... and stared at it as if he had seen it before... and in reality... he had... It was one of the books she had finished reading... but what it was doing on the table... he didn't know... She was not like him who would read a book again and again... Reading once was enough for her... and reading once made her take the characters and putting them inside a secret pocket in her heart...

"Didn't you sleep...?" She asked... standing somewhere in the dark staring at him... He could feel her gaze...

"I did... but I woke up..." He took another glass of crushed watermelon and handed it to her... She took a sip and her gaze was back on him... He knew that she wouldn't switch on the light until she felt like it... She always hated how the light pierced her eyes...

"What is love to you...?" He asked abruptly and he himself was surprised to realise what he had asked...

"I thought you already knew..." He could feel her nod gently and hear her take occasional sips from the glass... Cold watermelon juice during a scorching summer night seemed somehow right...

He could feel her gaze on him again as if she read his mind... He preferred blind conversations like this once in a while... and now... it seemed more than beneficial...

"I do know..." He replied trying to assess her expression... But it was hard for him in the dark too... No matter how well his eyes adjusted to the dark... he was no cat... "... I meant about what love mean to you now... when you're with me..."

"Hmm..." There was a long pause and it seemed as if she was deep in thought... After a while... he could hear the juice sliding down her throat and he assumed she was going to answer...

"It's like we're tied with a beautiful thread... not restricted or controlled in any manner... but more like linked... and it's not just you and me... There's God too... that energy we denote as God... you know... Linking us... you... me... and the God..."

It was his turn to think now... The darkness served the purpose well... He focused on a very abstract shape in the dark which he assumed was one of the branches of the tree outside and began his thought process...

"Do you have butterflies in your stomach...?" He himself had no clue why that question seemed relevant then and there... It was as if he was purely controlled by his thoughts...

"Not really..."

"Shouldn't you have it...? People in love have it... don't they...?"

"They do... but I don't... It's more like I'm at peace... you know... like when you're at home and you can wear anything you like... or eat anything that you crave... or take a shower only if you're up to... Our relationship is something like that for me... Not like butterflies in my stomach or tip toe excitement..."

"Hmm..." He gave it a thought... a deep one... "I like that actually... and I think I feel the same too..."

"Don't feel the same because I feel it... Just define it for yourself... and you'll be at peace..."

"It's my definition... and I like it..."

He could feel her smiling at his answer and vaguely see her nodding her head at him... She finished her drink and rinsed it... all in the dark as if she was an expert like a cat... Maybe that's what their love is supposed to be... A walk in the dark... but in a very familiar place called home that they see vision even in darkness... It was vision in blindness... and he loved the thought of it...

***

XXXIV

Conversation Thirty Four...

"People don't appreciate sincerity nowadays..." She said out of the blue... her eyes sparkling and her face frowned in deep angles... The topic came from thin air as if it had been part of the invisible air for quite too long... He knew she needed his undivided attention... now that she had actually voiced it out... It was like something coming out of the invisible air and forming several groups of symbols ending with a question mark... which also is a question mark at the end...

"We've had this conversation before... I know... But I guess I've more questions that aren't dead yet... or that refuse to die..."

He was glad he didn't ask anything new... When her face is like that... when she's deep in her thoughts... it was always better to give her the space and let it all come out... or else half of it would materialize back into the invisible world and would never see the daylight...

"Why do you think people don't accept sincerity nowadays...?"

He wasn't expecting that question... It was as if he had received a blow to his head... His fingers ran along the backbone of the book he was currently reading and he felt the worn-out part on which his fingers began picking on the edge...

Why wouldn't people appreciate sincerity...! It was a question she herself had answered... People aren't ready to do the hard work... They just want to be lazy... Lazy and still want the medal... That was what they wanted... He wanted to say... She knew the answer... he wanted to say... But none of it came along...

"It's not just laziness... is it...? It's some sort of jealousy as well... don't you think...?"

He wasn't expecting that... Jealousy was something he wasn't expecting... It was something new... Laziness was something that she had came up with... but jealousy... Who would be jealous... of their own children... Own... Owning... It was one of the dangerous words... he realised...

"None of the people want to see their children be better than them... they just want to be seen as the perfect person with perfect knowledge... and with unending resources... But when the children become better than them... they seem to go over the board... as if their kids are pirates walking them to the unending depths of the ocean..."

He was silent... the most silent he has ever been in his entire life... It was somewhere true... and there were stories in the past about parents getting jealous about their children... So... it wasn't entirely possible for the rest of the people to be jealous of somebody else's achievements...

"I'm tired of expecting that if we hold out an opinion... somebody powerful would come and make it happen... like they would sway their magic wand and everything would come back to normal..."

He wanted to ask why her pauses were long... why she got tired... but he knew... he got tired ages ago...

"No one's going to change anything for the better... are they...! The world has become hopeless... Completely dry and lost..."

The conversation led nowhere... he knew... It was more like an intrapersonal conversation... She was talking more to herself than to him... It happened once in a while... and he knew how frequent it happened to her... He waited... he waited for all of it to come out... but none of it came afterwards... It stopped... It stopped as if it never began... He felt it odd... as if he was watching a memory of hers out loud... Memories could be watched out loud... only memories could be done so... It was just like that...

"Do you think if I'm sincere people would push me down the stairs...?"

He didn't know... Maybe... Maybe not... It was not a question he could answer... It was something only time could answer... if time was willing to... of course... He stared at her blankly and she knew... Like always... she knew him now too... and she'll know him after too..."

***

XXXV

Conversation Thirty Five...

A kitten was sleeping... its purr vibrating her tummy where the kitten slept... A puppy was wagging its tail with its eyes glancing from the back of the book he was reading towards his fingers where he was holding a ball ready to be thrown for the puppy to fetch...

They had adopted both of them the last week... They had decided then and there that the orange kitten will be called Tiny and the white puppy with large black splotches will be called Blackie... They had both adopted the names wholeheartedly and have become family to them... Tiny took a while to own them while Blackie accepted them as their family immediately...

He threw the ball gently around the hall and the puppy wagged its tail and ran behind the ball... The kitten... on the other hand... slept peacefully through it...

Blackie came with the ball and dropped it before him... He smiled at him and threw the ball again... He slammed the book shut and looked at her as she read... She slammed the book shut and stared at him... He stared back at her eyes and she did the same... Neither of them had any words left to speak...

They stared for quite a while but neither of them began... It was he who wanted to ask something... more like confess his predictions about his own future if she were to leave... But he knew she wasn't going to... His own conflicting thoughts were at war inside his own head... She could see it in his eyes... She wanted to know who would win... who would decide the future predictions tonight... who would know what was in her heart... She wondered if he could read her mind... and he... as if to confirm that he can... had a different expression altogether... He knew her happiness was with him and Blackie and Tiny... This was her home... and this will be her home... This is where she had her rebirth and this will be the place where she breathes her last... He had known it all... and he had seen it all... and he had felt it all... and he still do...

He closed his eyes and took a deep breath... then looked at her and smiled... This was all he needed... but he needed it quite a lot too... His insecurities could be made into a list and it might well reach the moon... He wanted to take it away from him and burn it into ashes and let it go... But not all mental issues could be cured that way... He knew... and she knew... and they both knew... He could handle her well... and she could handle him well... Maybe this was what peace felt like after all... to be in the arms of the ones whom we love... and whom we can understand... and who can understand us back...

She smiled back at him and nodded as she took her book... He too followed her example and began reading... The kitten was still asleep... and the puppy still wagged its

MAALU...

tail for the next throw...

***

XXXVI

Conversation Thirty Six...

"I don't know what to do... I don't know if I should stay or go abroad..." he said abruptly... his tone rising and falling quickly as if he was panicking...

She stared longingly at the book that was on her lap... she wanted it to be over... this discussion that took her brain out of her skull... this conversation that prevented her from thinking straight...

"You tell me... you tell me where to go... you tell me if I should stay or go..." Tiny purred slightly and jumped up over her book... trying to be comfortable... She picked up the book and Tiny almost smirked like a devil as she lied down and slept...

"I... I can't tell you what to do..." she said finally... stroking Tiny's fur... "That's your choice..." she didn't want to be the one who decided his fate... and she didn't want to be the one who ended their future... The time kept running as if it stopped for no one... especially for them... She was getting older... and so was he... They had to decide... they had to convince... Convincing was the tough job...

"I will go to Canada... study well... get a job... and take you there... How's that...?" he said looking over his written down notes about different places and the scholarships... The pages kept fluttering as if this conversation would never end... It gave her a headache...

"Sure... I would love that..." and yet again... she was the damsel in distress... just as how her parents had trained her to be... But the blames never imprinted on them... It was as if the blames would somehow bounce off of them as how a raindrop bounces off a lotus leaf...

"Will you be okay...?"

"What...?"

"Will you be okay...?"

"Ye... yes... I would be okay... It's you who need to be in focus... You go there... study well... come home... and take me with you... Do you get that...?"

"Yes ma'am..."

She kept stroking Tiny... She was fast asleep and comfortable too... She kept looking at Tiny as if she would help her escape into a fantasy world where the pain would... fade... She didn't want him to go... She didn't want to miss him... But he had to... and she knew it well... as much as he did... It's not like he is going to go forever... He will be back... He knew it... She knew it... But the pain doesn't... Pain doesn't know that...

There were million little things she wanted to tell him... Even this decision wasn't decided on a whim... He called and called almost all the people he knew... He asked her a thousand times for what he should do... and she refused to decide on his behalf... His decision was his and his alone... she would say... And this was the decision he finally reached and she was happy for him...

"You should take Blackie too..." she suggested looking at the puppy at his feet... "It would be too much with both of them here when you're gone... and besides... you're his favourite... I don't want to deal with his temper tantrums when you're gone..."

"Is that so Blackie...?" he asked...

"Woof..."

"It will be tricky coming with me Blackie... You sure you want to come...?"

"Woof..."

"So... it's settled then..."

She smiled at both of them... It wouldn't be too bad for her and Tiny to be here alone... And besides... she won't be alone... She would have Tiny... and a couple of good books... and beanbag... and coffee... and chocolate... and blanket... She won't be alone... And he would come back soon... There's nothing to worry about... nothing...

"You okay...?"

"Yeah..."

"You sure...?"

"I'll be..."

They held their pinky fingers... Both of them knew they would reach back home... reach back into a circle and start a new one... But the pain didn't know... And it hurts...

***

XXXVII

Conversation Thirty Seven...

When the day I shall die comes...
Let my absence soothe you into a deep slumber...
Devoid of dreams and hopes...
Let my absence tell you stories of our memories...
Let it grab your hands by your fingers...
And lead you into the darkness where I shall wait...
And let your fear fade into nothingness...
That we both shall become one day...
And I must say my dear...
What I am is not you...
And what you are is not me...
But when the day I shall die comes...
Let us be nothing but a handful of ashes in an urn...

He kept reading the poem again and again as if it would not end any time soon... It kept replaying in his brain as if it was a broken record... When the day she shall die comes... It was painful even to read... and torture to imagine this... He kept running his eyes over the lines with what he assumed was his brain refusing to accept the mortality that one day... both of them has to face...

What was romance to Freud...? What was psychology to Plath...? What was death to God...? Nothing... simply nothing... nothing more than a part of life... and definitely nothing more than a speck of dust... Shakespeare once asked so bravely... *What's in a name? That which we call a rose... By any other name would smell as sweet...* What was in his name... and what was in hers too...? Names and existence meant nothing despite how much meaning they tried to thrust it upon them... His eyes... his brain... his heart... every organ in his body... everything felt like draining from him... squeezed dry out of him...

He turned around and looked at her... the poet who had conjured up these lines out of thin air... She was no poet in his mind... she was more than a poet... even a magician who could conjure up words from thin air... How could any of this was possible for her... what was the secret she held in her heart... like Shelley's Skylark and Keats' Nightingale... Oh how desperately both of them try to possess their birds and failed miserably in the end... only to realise that humans could not possess even their own life... even their own soul...

The time when she dies... the moment when he realises that she is not permanent in his life... the moment he realises they are not permanent in this world... What are their names in this world...! Have they ever carved their names on the bark of any tree...? Did they sketch out a map where the world could find their names once written down on the face of the earth...? Was it necessary for the world to find them... or did he just want them to know they did exist... once upon a time...

She kept watching him intently... not a single word came out of her lips... He wished desperately... if she would tell him something... He knew... from the words... She was not planning to leave him alone to suffer... She was not letting him leave her alone either... It was as they once planned... If it's early or late... they would journey to the other world hand-in-hand... If it were just them... he would be merrier still...

"Would you tell me something...?" he asked out of the blue...

She smiled a yes...

"How deeply you love me...! Tell me how to measure it..."

"Measure it by loving me back..."

Ghost of which poet possessed their tongue they do not know... but the words remained truer to their core...

***

XXXVIII

Conversation Thirty Eight...

"What would affect you more... me leaving you... or my death...?" she asked abruptly... He wasn't expecting such a question... he wasn't expecting a question at all... She knew the answer well... even before it would come out of his lips... Even though... listening to his words somehow assured a lot many things than simply assuming the answer...

"In either case... your absence will affect me drastically... It would tear me into pieces... It would kill me too..."

She stayed silent trying to bring out more from him... but he still stared at her eyes as if no words could explain what he actually felt... And it was true... Feelings could never be explained through mere words... no matter how creative of a word was developed...

"I know all of this is cliché... I know you're not satisfied with what I've told you... Maybe that's the curse of language... The more languages we learn... the more incapable we become at explaining what we feel..."

She nodded absentmindedly into the air... It made sense... What he said made sense... She knew exactly how she would feel if the names in the question were replaced... She knew how much she would be broken if he were to suddenly disappear from the world as if he never existed... It would be more painful than an artery popping... an artery that connected both their hearts... It's hard to explain... but they knew... both of them knew well...

"Promise me... you'll never leave me like that..." he said...

"I promise..." she whispered...

***

XXXIX

Conversation Thirty Nine...

It was cold and dark and dull... Every now and then they could hear someone coughing or cursing the rain... Her eyes have swollen dangerously and have transformed into two huge red spheres... Her head felt heavy and her mind have gone blank on its own... She had been crying for so long as if her appearance didn't clarify it enough... She should have comforted him instead... He was his friend after all... She should have been there for him... instead it was he comforting her... She felt embarrassed of herself... of her emotions ricocheting out of her eyes and her heart... and from every pore on her body... She couldn't comfort him... she knew... and felt anger build up against herself... Instead... all she did was cry the previous night to sleep... and cry again in the morning... and cry more at night... And all those crying had exhausted her...

"I never knew I loved him as much as I do now..." she said out of the blue... "I knew I loved you... and I knew I saw him as your friend... and one of my friends with whom I spoke very less... but... but..."

She knew it was an accident and the damage was done below waist... He was thrown out of the bike onto the road and he had broken his bones... Every time his face came to her... her eyes would well up...

"Did I see him as my little boy...? Is that why I feel this way...? He was my little boy though... Even though he's your friend and he's almost the same age as me... he was my little boy... he was our little boy... Wasn't he...?

He didn't answer her immediately... He was not able to decipher her message completely... It broke his heart too... to know what had happened to his friend... and how his partner is reacting to it... It was as if both of his loved ones are hurt at the same time and he couldn't do anything to help any of them...

When will we see him...? Would we go soon...? How's he now...?

His mind kept echoing these lines back to him... even though it wasn't his voice he heard... but hers... He could almost feel her words... almost catch her voice in his hands... feel every vibration... feel every broken part...

"He will be fine... I know you're hurt... I know you're suffering..."

"I am... There's no us without him... It's because of him that we met... It's because he stood by the corridors and the veranda talking to me that you began talking with me... and I talked to you... And that's not just it... He's our friend... and it hurts... it breaks my heart..."

And fresh hot tears spilled out from the corners of her eyes... She kept wondering from where all these tears were coming from... She was after all a dried raisin... She became still for a moment and hurriedly picked up a pen and a paper and began scribbling something out... The paper was yellow in colour and of a poor quality... He assumed it was some neglected backside of a bill... After scribbling something down so frantically she began crying out loud... screaming so loudly as if she was desperately trying to let out all of her pain... She cried so much that she couldn't stay up much longer... her head hurt as it got heavier... her eyes warned her to pop out of her sockets if she continued this... But she couldn't stop... She couldn't stop unless she saw him...

***

It was a while until she fell asleep on the couch crying... She ate a little dinner... which he had to force feed her... but then she wasn't hungry... She slept crying too much that he feared she might catch a cold by the morning... It was freezing cold monsoon after all... He took the yellow bill and began reading...

The cigarette smoke stains the room...
As if it's marking the black room...
Sucking life out of me for you...
So that I could trade it back to you...
Your pain breaks my heart...
Split it into two...
And I wish I could stop it...
Just by being in your place...
Instead of you...
I admit...
I'm not fond of the pain of broken bones...
I'm not fond of the stink of hospital rooms...
I'm not fond of the green bedsheets and the white walls...
I'm not fond of the nurses or the white coats that accompany them...
But I'll... in a matter of seconds...

If given an option... would switch places...
Because out of all people I should know this...
Endless tears hurt more than numbness...
And a broken heart hurts more than broken bones...

He read it once... and then twice... The first time he couldn't read it all... His eyes began filling up and his vision was blurred... It was not like he could see the second time... He kept reading... and then wiping his eyes... and reading again... and then wiping again... All that came to his mind was his helmet coloured in an American flag theme and evening long conversations at the public ground...

***

XL

Conversation Forty...

While you lay unconscious...

Trying to keep your bright eyes open...

Trying to hold on for more days... months... and years...

So... you could see us all... for the rest of your life...

Do you know how many times I heard your voice...?

Do you know how many times I listened to you sing...?

Do you know how many times I looked at your photographs...?

Do you know how many times I listened to the band singing...

"I'll be there for you..."?

If I knew how to count beyond my ten fingers and my ten toes...

I did tell you it's been more than that...

Can you hear my heart screaming...

As you lie... your eyes closed... breathing...?

Can you hear it breaking when I lose hope...?

And can you hear it gluing itself back together when the hope is renewed...?

Do you know how much I want to go back in time...

And trade my life for yours...?

My heart breaks painfully...

More than you can imagine...

The pain building up bit by bit...

But severe enough...

That I guess it would burst soon and everything will be over once and for all...

But no... it won't... the pain grows steadily... gradually...

Wish I could trade my life for yours...

Trade it with a smiling face...

Trade it with a happy heart...

Wish I could take your pain away...

Just to see you smile...

Just to see you sing again...

Sing with all your heart...

So... the world could hear you over and over again...

I can't stop writing... because this isn't poetry anymore...

This isn't art anymore...

This is just me...

Crying on and on...

For you... just for you...

And she began crying endlessly... Despite his false hopes... she knew what was going to happen... Their friend was not going to come back... and at times... she kept screaming internally at the wall... as if she was screaming at God, Himself...

I trusted you... I trusted you'd bring him back... I thought you'd bring him back...

But there were no replies back... The wall remained silent and unmoving... He hadn't cried yet... It scared her so much... Why wasn't he crying...? Why wasn't he shedding tears...? She looked at him as he planned their trip to his house the next day... so that they could tell him their final good bye...

A number of phone calls later... and thousands of questioning and answering... he switched off his phone and threw it aimlessly onto the table... She got up and squeezed in with him on his beanbag... something they would normally refuse to do... She hugged him as hard as she could as if she was cracking his bones as well... The whole night... the whole dark night... they cried through... None of them slept... Because... the moment they closed their eyes... his face... his smile... his voice... everything popped up... He's no more... He won't sing for them anymore... and they couldn't sing to him either... even though they weren't professional singers like him...

***

XLI

Conversation Forty One...

She was fast asleep as he came to the living room after doing the dishes... She hadn't eaten much that night... She had cried too much... She was finally slept after all the exaggerated emotions of hers... He was his friend... and she loved him dearly... There was no comparison in that... There was nothing to compare... They saw him the way they knew how to...

There was a book lying open over her chest and a pen barely clinging to her fingers... It looked like a diary... She was not fond of diary entries... he knew... but this sure did look like a diary... He didn't think much of it and took it out of her hands to keep it closed on the table... It was hard to let her grip loose... but he did take it out of her hands... He was about to keep it on the table when the first line struck him... It was a letter... and he knew who it was addressed to... He couldn't help but read...

Dear friend...

It's been a day since you've gone... I don't know where you went... but is that place a good one for you... better than here...? Are there spirits who love you genuinely...? I hope you're happy there... I hope you're not scared or feeling lonely... Can you see us from wherever you are...? Can you feel how much we love you...? None of our love was fake... despite the less frequency at which we spoke...

Your friend is scared at how I'm behaving now... I think he's worried for me... I've cried too much... and still it seems I can't end this... I've been asking him if we could join you there... but... he wouldn't let me... He says you won't like it... He knew you better than I did... and I bet he is right... You wouldn't like that... You wanted everyone around you to be happy... Your smile always made us happy too...

I guess you're still smiling from wherever you're... I've never seen you without a smile... I don't want to see you otherwise either... But I saw you lying motionless on the floor... It hurt me too much... I wanted to sit with you... hold your cheek... tell you who all have come to see you... I wanted you to meet that new face too... his other friend... and tell you he could never replace you... that you don't have to worry about us forgetting you... because that's never going to happen...

Last night... he reminded me of our dream... of a little house by the river... with a puppy and kitten... There was an extra addition to it... There's an extra room when he told me about it the last night... That's for you... That room is for you... We'll keep it tidy always... and we'll keep it ready always... We know you'd visit some day... at times... It's like Chandler and Monica saving a room for their Joey... You know... you were our Joey... someone who valued every single relationship more than anything...

I didn't know much about you... and still I couldn't stop crying... I'm crying as I write this... and I can picture myself crying every morning and every night for you... I don't think I can get over this as easily as I thought I could... I kept asking him a lot... literally begged him if we could come with you... be he didn't let me... He told me you wouldn't like that... Even after you've gone... you still love us too much... How the hell can you do that...? How did you love us unconditionally...? I always wanted a brother... a friend... who never judged... and you were that for me... I feel like a big chunk of me left me when you were gone... I lost someone who never judged me... who accepted me the way I was... just as how your friend is doing... But you were my brother... you were family... How could you leave...?

I would write you letters more often... Your friend asked me to write a book about you... Maybe that's a good idea... You'll be here with us then... in our memories... and in our heart... and even after we join you... you'd still be here... immortal in these lines...

We were the perfect tripod... a same religion but different caste tripod... Despite what our parents had thought about castes and stuff... we were always together... We were so perfect... We were more than perfect... I can't imagine you're gone... It kills me... But I'll keep my promises to you and your friend... I'll keep writing letter for you... and I'll write a book for you... Always...

With lots and lots of love...

He closed the book and hugged it closer to his chest and began crying silently... He didn't want to wake her up... She had slept tired... and if he did wake her up... she would only cry more... His tears drenched the edges of the book...

"If only you knew... how much we loved you..."

***

XLII

Conversation Forty Two...

The days kept passing and their pain seemed like it was only getting worse... Both of them were broken forever and there was nothing that could turn the wheels of time and bring him back... and make things as it was... She was sitting on his lap... cuddling to his chest as she wrote in her diary... She wasn't bothered if he was really reading it or not... Maybe she wanted him to read through...

Dear friend...

It's the third day after you've left... It seems like the time isn't at all moving... like we are both stuck... and for some reason we couldn't move further... Your friend still has his reins over his body... in spite of the sadness that is breaking him from within... But I can barely make sense of my dreams and my reality... It's as if I'm lost somewhere in between... I could barely make sense of the time... the dreams... the reality... or any feeling that a normal person should feel... should comprehend... I've somehow stopped crying... That seems to make your friend feel a little better... He had also asked me to tell him whatever I feel... but my heart is beyond any feelings... The only thing I can feel is a clenching pain in my chest... as if I'm going to die and join you in afterlife...

What would I tell your worrying friend...? Can you help me...? He thinks I'm lying when I'm saying I've no thoughts about you or that I cannot feel anything... He thinks I'm lying so as to stop him from worrying about me... Besides... I can't cry... No... not anymore... I've promised you that I'd look after your friend... and if I cry... he'll break apart... I'm terrified... I don't know what to do... I'm so scared that it makes me go mad...

I dreamt of you last night... I don't remember what I dreamt... but I swear I saw your smiling face... and I heard your lovely voice... and I felt your touch as if I was riding behind your bike like once you took me... All these memories bring tears... but I'm trying not to cry... I can't... If I keep crying... I don't think I'll ever stop...

A lot many people cried that day for you... We know you don't like to see us crying... but tell me... how will we stay happy when you're gone...? You know how much it hurts us... you did see how still and angry and dangerous I was when we came to your house... I always wanted to see your house... but not like this... We haven't talked much... have we...? You might probably wonder what the hell is wrong with me... I wish I could tell you... but I don't know myself... My brain is trying its best to keep me safe from the pain... you know... like defence mechanisms you've learnt in psychology... but it only got itself so confused that it can't remember what is real and what is not...

He's with me as I'm writing this... He's reading it over my shoulder... and I can feel his eyes get blurry as he passes through those lines... I'll show him some nice movies and series... that you probably might have seen already... I'll take him to movies if new ones come... And when we go... I want you to come with us... We'll save a seat for you... You can then brag to your new friends above... about the new movies you saw with us... And also... we would like to spend time in places you've been... near the public playground... and I want you to join us... To see that we are together and that we aren't going to split up... because look at you... you glued us together... how could we ever break that...! And I want you to stay with us always... I know it's a pretty selfish wish... but I hope you'd stay... We miss you... we miss you greatly... I hope you know...

With lots and lots of love...

He hugged her closer to his chest and tightened his grip around her... and began crying... She was numb... She could barely say or even cry... She couldn't feel his fingers or his arms like she used to... Nevertheless... they stayed like that for a very long time...

***

XLIII

Conversation Forty Three...

Dear friend...

It has become weird how I barely talk to your friend... It's like I don't want to wake up... or even breathe... He told me that he felt scared more than getting sad by losing you... I don't know what went wrong with me... With me... I guess... a part of me died... and that part needs justice... It wants to lie down... sleep forever... and never wake up... But half of me is still alive... and that part of me needs to keep getting up... and has to be fed... and has duties to do... And all that people see is this alive part just because I breathe...

Your friend tries his best to understand the situation... give me as much space as he can... and still tries to look after me as much as he can... But even he sees only the alive part... and the scare you gave him is too focused on whatever's that's left alive... he doesn't see the dead part... I feel very sad that I can't provide him the comfort he deserves... You were his friend after all... and we are the ones who barely talked... I can't imagine the pain he goes through... It kills me to think that I've become completely useless and incompetent right now... It kills me that I can't be what he wants me to be...

The part that's still alive tries its best to move on like how a normal person should do... tries its best to keep away the tears... and tries to smile and push through every waking day... but the part that's dead... it's weighing down the other... and it's as if I'm dragging the dead weight along... If I were to ask a sane person what I should do... the sane person would ask me to lose the dead weight... But I don't think I can... That dead weight was the happiest part of me... where I was this happy bright child in between you... holding both of your hands... having a family that she never had... And with you gone... it's half gone... I'm not good at math... but I know I'm right here...

I even tried laughing today watching a series with your friend... but it brought me back to tears... and I cried... hours of not crying... I cried... It was like I was defeated... and every single time I cry... I feel bad for your friend... I tell him that his choice was bad... defective in reality... even though me choosing him was perfect... Because if it were anyone else in his place... they would've labelled me as a slut... and besties stealing girlfriends are a trend... I've got the best person I could ever possibly dream of... or even deserve to be honest... and look at how I treat him... I must be the most horrible person alive on this planet... A half dead... half alive person... Does that even make sense...?

Your friend deserved better... you know... At times I wish if he had taken your warning and saved himself... I'm a lost cause way before I reached him... He knows that himself... He tells me that everyone ruined me and he has got the worst part of me... He doesn't mean it in a negative way though... I do love him... with all my heart... and I desperately want to be there for him... But like I told you... Half of me is already dead when you left... I didn't even know that my soul was connected to you and your friend at the same time... I thought that could happen only once... We were like a triangle... or a tripod leaning on each other to support a canvas with a big picture... But you broke midway... and now this big picture had fallen down with a huge thud... I don't think two of us are strong enough to hold it upright... You were our backbone... you were our pillar... and you've left us alone to face this cruel misunderstanding piece of world... I'm thinking of tattooing my chest... a blown away dandelion perhaps... close to my heart... It's you... you're the blown away dandelion... Dandelions are supposed to be wishes coming true... but it has turned rogue... Meanings have changed... and the tables have turned... I've only one wish now... When it's time for us to join you... I hope it's you who come for us... no one else... not even God... You... I hope you'll come smiling in your bright red car... honking... smiling... taking our fear of death away... and take us by our hands... and take us back home... I hope you'll be the one who comes... and so we will meet again...

With lots and lots of love...

He read that too with blurry eyes... These were not letters just for his friend... even though it's addressed to him... It was for both of them... She was desperately trying to communicate how she feels... but failing each and every time she does it... not able to communicate exactly how she feels... It ached his heart... and it broke into tears... She had asked once... how long do they have to go on like this... half of them dead... and them desperately trying to hold onto their dear life... Life has in fact lost its colour and meaning... He wished he knew the answer of what they both were supposed to be doing... But it seems... he was as lost as her... They were both lost in the sea of busy people... a lot of them who had already forgotten him... and a majority who never met him...

***

XLIV

Conversation Forty Four...

Dear friend...

It's been six days since you've gone... It's like I'm counting both our days... looking for how long we'll keep up this war between our own thoughts... I've finally stopped crying... but not completely though... I'd cry today... just once... when I saw your video where you were singing one of my favourite songs... It's a small song... and it's quite easy to learn the lyrics... so I watched the video and learnt the lyrics singing along with you... Singing along with you made me feel like I'm wrapped up in a warm blanket in a cold rainy morning... half asleep... half awake... I felt like you had an arm wrapped around my shoulder... and next to you Freud was sitting and listening... Out of politeness you don't comment on my out of place tunes... but he was singing along with me... and both of our out of place tunes were annoying you... It was fun...

I know I can't see you or hear you... because I don't read frequencies that cats and dogs can... so... yeah... tough luck... But

I believe that you can see me and hear me and read over my shoulder what I'm writing... I believe that you can see him too... and I believe that you're watching over him... It's funny that most people say I'm the cry baby and that I need help... which I don't deny... but if you ask me who needs to be protected... I'd say it's your friend... I'd be happy if you're watching over him for me rather than being with me... But that doesn't mean I don't want you or that you can skip on me on your visits... I'll be waiting too...

A few days earlier I'd told him that I had to dig deeper into your memories for me to recover because that was the only way I knew how to recover... and he questioned me harshly when I began talking about suicide... I really wanted to sleep... you know... I'd a life that was far from colourful... I don't blame him... He was worried... He asked me a lot of things... which I'm not elaborating here... I don't want you to be sad... but mostly... if what you said was right and you were actually watching us... you might already know this... I wrote my suicide note as if I'm writing down my will before I die... and gave it to him... so that if some day my suicide goes unplanned and impulsive... he would have a heads up... And it made him sad... I promised that I'd stay with him even if I'm gone... like you do... I even convinced him to join me... so that we both could join you... but he was afraid of pain... He couldn't... and so I had to stay... I miss you greatly... I don't think there's a tool to measure it...

I was angry at everyone except you when you left... and I was especially angry at God for taking you despite all the promises I gave Him... But your friend... he convinced me otherwise... I don't know how he did it... but he did... He asked me to fill the pages with your memories so you'd live with us... among us... like how you used to... It was hard to stay alive after you left... I just wanted to leave this miserable world and come running over to you... wherever you are... but like I said... I had to stay for your friend... or you'll be angry at me for leaving him alone... I'm sure of it... And every single day... I'm trying my best to get up from my bed... do things I usually do... push through life... and keep a straight head so that when your friend calls... I could talk to him... I'm not saying I recovered... or that I am on the path of healing... because I'd cry today... but I'm trying... trying my best not to let go... keeping the promise I gave you when we came to see you...

I don't know if he is counting the days like I am... I never asked... I'm not yet smiling either... so talking itself is a task for me... But I'm crossing out the days and keeping count as if I'm one of those prisoners carving tally marks on the walls... waiting to get out... I'm not good at counting... but I guess this... I'll be counting this...

I don't want to forget you... and I don't want others who knew you to forget you... and I don't want the world who never knew to be ignorant of your existence... I don't know how long I'll write letters to you... but as long as I'm alive... your memory will still be with me... Even if I forget your name and face when I'm old and miserable... I'll always remember that I loved you... and that I still love you... I love you... and I hope you'll come back soon and take us with you... I never got to have a long journey with you... so you kind of owe me here... I'll be waiting... Always...

With lots and lots of love...

It was one of the longest letters she had written so far and a voice inside him told him that she wasn't going to stop writing letters any time soon... He gently held the notebook closer to his chest and stared at the cloudy night sky... He could barely see any stars... But deep inside him... he knew... he's with them... Just as he thought that very thought... a gentle breeze blew and his hair fluttered over his forehead... he looked over his left shoulder... from where the breeze came... and smiled... As he smiled fresh tears spilled out from the corner of his eyes... He knew in that moment... both of them weren't going to forget him... and that he's going to be with them forever...

***

XLV

Conversation Forty Five...

Dear friend...

It's the seventh day after you've gone... I still can't handle the grief of your departure... It's like... one moment you're there... and the next... you're gone... You got hurt before my birthday and you left after my birthday... perfectly enveloping my birthday in... in such a way that I've lacked any interest of celebrating it in future... I'll always remember the dates... I'll always remember how I felt when your friend called me and told me you got hurt... I'll always remember how much helpless I felt and how much I cried hoping you'd wake up to see us and would tell something funny like you used to... I'll always remember how much I wanted to smack on your head for being so careless so that the next time you'd remember us when you drive... I'll always remember how I prayed constantly for you to come back and see us and talk to us... I'll always remember how I felt when a batch mate announced in the group that sadly you've left... and I'll always remember how much anger I felt to the whole world and God and everyone but you...

If you ask me whether counting days help... it doesn't actually... But if you ask why I'm doing it... I don't have an answer for it either... Maybe counting does help in some ways that I cannot fathom... It's like counting sheep to fall asleep technique... I'm counting days so that I could fall asleep... and join wherever you're...

I still think about all the pain you went through... all the broken bones you've had to feel... all the infection spreading... I wonder what your thoughts were... Was the pain too much that you wanted to leave... or was the pain of leaving us too much that you wanted to come back...? Some movies show us that people see their memories and loved ones before they go... I wonder if you saw us too... along with your family... or at least your friend... I hope you saw him... I hope you heard his voice in the hospital corridors begging everyone if he could see you... I hope you heard his tears and his helplessness... I hope you heard how much we all cried for you... I'm not asking you to be sad... but I want you to know that we loved you with all our heart... Us... me and your friend... we don't know how to love otherwise... We've always been told by others that loving too much can be painful... and we knew the risks too... Because most people we loved... they left us for better ones... But you... you are the only one who actually stayed and I almost thought it perfect... but... God took you... tore you from us mercilessly... just to remind us that nothing is perfect and the world is unfair... That's why I was angry at God... He could have taken someone else and lessened the pain and taught us that... but you... by taking you... he tore us into helpless bits... desperately trying to lean on each other... and supporting each other...

I've heard others say that when their parents die that's when they feel like an orphan... no matter how old they were when they die... But for me... you leaving us made me feel like an *orphan... It's like I've no one to complain to if your friend becomes mischievous... I'm not saying that he will... but before you left... I had you to complain... I saw you more like my friend and an elder brother I never had... a guardian of sort... I know it's not fair to ask of you... we barely talked... I don't think I do have the right to ask that from you either... I'm drowning in a lot of guilt... you know... I know you know...*

If ever comes the day when I'll marry your friend... which I hope does come true with all my relatives beside me... will you hold my hand and walk with me...? Will you join us on the stage and be with us always...? Will you come visit us often...? I know I'm pushing the boundaries here... but... can you take birth on this planet once again... as our baby...? I don't know if it's even right asking you this... I don't know what's right and wrong anymore... I feel like I'm completely lost... But if you take birth as such... we promise we'll love you as much as we loved you in this life... with all our heart... and hopefully... we all can go visit your parents once in a while... I hope it will comfort them more... They would be able to know that their baby boy hasn't gone... I don't know what I'm talking... I feel like I'm talking nonsense... I don't know... But whatever nonsense I'm talking right now... I know that one thing I told you isn't nonsense... We both loved you with all our heart... and we'll continue to do so no matter what...

With lots and lots of love...

The letters kept growing in numbers day by day... and his guess wasn't in vain... He knew she wasn't going to stop writing... at least not any time soon... Time doesn't heal scars... it either makes it severe or it makes it bearable... it doesn't actually heal... He didn't know what was in store for them... was it going to be worse or was it going to be better...? He didn't know... He was just looking at the sky... holding the notebook closer to his chest... and hoping for the best... He believed God knew what was best for them... His faith wasn't gone yet... He felt a palm resting on his shoulder... which was not hers... but still familiar... He didn't turn around to look... he just knew who it was...

***

XLVI

Conversation Forty Six...

I don't look at the dates anymore... like a normal person does... I'm simply counting it like that makes more sense than looking at dates... It's the eighth day since you have left... I can literally picture myself saying that it has been eight days when someone asks me what the date is... or what day it's... I've not been able to think straight anymore... I've gone out of my ways to keep myself a straight-faced human... I don't like this version of me... this version that suppresses all the emotions just to stop from crying and becoming numb in the process... I don't like it...

I do try my best not to cry though... but you know me... How long do you think I'll go on like this...? I find time to cry when your friend isn't here... I bet he already knows... He's just pretending he doesn't know because I'm not ready to talk about it... I try to cry as silently as possible... holding my nose and mouth closed... like how I was taught from the young age... It's quite effective... Your body starts reacting to the lack of oxygen and silently shuts off... the whole tear system shuts down... and you wipe your face... and your out of the bathroom before you know it... I also try listening to the running water in the bathroom... The running water calms me... not in a way it calms normal people... I guess you know it by now... I'm not normal... It calms me in a way that... it helps me think that I'm drowning... but I'm not struggling against it... simply drowning... only to float back up lifeless... like a neon orange life jacket... Does that even make sense...? I guess in some ways it does... You know... like it's the life jacket's duty to save the person... and I'm like the life jacket here... saving your friend from drowning... and not once does the life jacket ever asks to be saved... It only saves people after people after people... I wonder if the life jacket gets tired... I wonder if I would get tired...

I don't know why it's me who's writing these letters to you and not your friend... Maybe it's because I'm his sponge too... and not simply a life jacket... Maybe I'm absorbing his emotions and writing it down... Maybe I'm just a medium for him to communicate to you... You were the medium who set us together... now I'm the medium keeping both of you together... I don't know why we both have the same roles... I don't know why He took you first from us... I don't seem to know anything at all... It's like shouting into the void... like how Gus says... I don't know if you've ever watched the movie... I don't think you've... You weren't a person of romance and tragedy... where you...? I can't picture you like that...

Do you remember our chats when I told you that you're the positive energy who comes late...? You were very happy to know that... You indeed were everybody's positive energy... Now you're gone... God took you from us... I don't know about the others... but for me... You were the only positivity... in a pool of negativity that I had to endure on a daily basis... and now I'm holding onto life as if I'm holding onto the last straw... I'm not saying your friend isn't positive… but he's different… You were literally the rainbow to my storms and your friend is more like the crayon imitation of it… Now in your absence… he had become literal grey clouds and sky… not the crayon version… but the original ones… I hate how grief change people into their worst… and I hate how unpredictable grief is… Are there colours up there too… wherever you're…? Do you like colours… or do colours hurt your eyes like it hurts mine…? I know I'm asking questions whose answers I'll never receive… But I like asking questions to you… If some day you have answers… please do come in my dreams and let me know… I know I should have asked these when you were here… and I regret I never asked these… I hope you're still listening and it's not too late… It's a shout in the void… but I know you're listening… I love you… We love you…

With lots and lots of love…

The night only kept growing darker and darker… The moon was invisible and the stars hid themselves… She didn't enjoy his company much nor did she want him to hug her or even comfort her… He could understand these things… He knew exactly how she felt too… He didn't know if the Chinese was right about the red thread of fate connecting just two souls… he felt that it connected these three together… and now… these two felt empty without the third one… Void… just huge black empty void… A void that has no beginning nor end… A void that can't be measured in any sort of manner… A void that just sucked life out of them like a black hole…

***

XLVII

Conversation Forty Seven...

Dear friend...

I have taken a break from God and I have become plugging my ears to Taylor Swift songs... like Mad Max from Stranger Things after Billy's death... She wasn't listening to Taylor Swift... but you get the idea... I've plugged my ears with Imagine Dragons as well... these two somehow speak to me in ways I cannot fathom... Your friend would not appreciate if I say that I took a break from God... I don't know if such things even make sense... but I'm definitely taking a break from God...

I prayed to God to bring you back... you know... even if your parents found it difficult to look after you... I promised him if you just came back... we would look after you... But... He turned a blind eye at us... But this letter isn't about complaining...

It's the eleventh day after you've left... and this is how drastic I've turned into... Controlling emotions will only eventually kill me... I don't know if your friend knows... I have never told him... it never seemed important...

I read this quote by Sylvia Plath the other day... "And so... it seems I must always write you letters that I can never send..." It's a classic irony... I'm writing you these letters which I know I'll never be able to send... But somehow... I know... you're reading them... I don't know how it makes you feel... I don't know if it makes you feel anything at all... I don't know if feelings are so below you that you've found the freedom that mortal life never gave you... Funeral is not for the dead... it's for the living... I've heard this from somewhere... I don't know if it's the exact same lines and that's why I'm not quoting them... and for some reason it's true...

Oh... I've began watching the series Young Sheldon... *You told me ages ago to watch it and see if I like it... and I do like it... and for some apparent reason it reminds me of you... There's no character in that series that resembles you... but still it reminds me of you... and I feel like you're with me...*

The days I'm counting... it feels like ages ago that you've gone... but when I'm counting... it's been only eleven days... a little more than a week... The void your absence creates is too much that I've lost sense about my surroundings... Your friend knows... and he's worried... But there's nothing much I can do... I've suppressed as much as I could and I've put on makeup to hide my dark circles and I've begun smiling to hide the nights I've cried under the bedsheet... Eleven days... it's just a little more than a week...

I hope you are reading all these letters... and I hope you do understand these... I don't know any other method of communicating to you better than writing... I'm writing letters to you as much as possible and I don't know when it will stop... I don't know if it ever will stop... I hope it doesn't... I don't want you to feel lonely or feel that we have stopped thinking about you... I don't think we ever will... I don't think we are fit for this century either... let alone this world... But if God kept us alive...

I think He just wants us to suffer... I don't know... I don't know about God... I'm just... I shouldn't be talking about this... Until next time...

With lots and lots of love...

Days passing by didn't make the pain any lesser or even tolerable... Not crying wasn't very effective either... He held the notebook closer to his chest like he always did... It made him feel that he was hugging both of them close...

***

XLVIII
Conversation Forty Eight...

"It's been 19 days..." she whispered as she looked out at the cold and dark sky... There were no stars and no moon... The clouds enveloped whatever that lit the dark sky... It's been said many a times that people who have left the material world would pop up in the sky as stars... and at times... they would stay back waiting for their loved ones to come... She didn't know what to believe... whom to trust... All she had was her hypothesis...

"You're still counting...?" he asked...

"Yes..." There was a huge pause... All the movies they watched... all the Netflix binging they did... was all just a distraction... for how long... neither of them knew... Her heart felt at ease though... unlike before... The pain began hiding itself inside her... not bothering her much... not resurfacing... just silently observing... numb and silent... "I don't think I'll ever stop..."

"I was afraid of that…" he said… staring at the darkened sky… The sky was merciless as before… and the world seemed to be ending…

"Do you think he's watching us… and that he's happy…?"

"I would love to think so…"

"I hope he's at peace now…"

He couldn't answer that… He believed he was at peace… He wouldn't want to believe in any other way… Both of them still couldn't think of him without tears and both of their brains seemed to somehow reject the truth just to smile and push through… They would laugh too occasionally… talking about him… his voice and his jokes… but… deep within… the ache still remained…

"I hope he's at peace… and that he's safe…" she whispered into the night sky… "I'm not supposed to say this… but I hope he comes back… just once… so that we could tell him how much we love him… we could tell him things we never said…"

"He knows…"

"It feels like a lie… I never told him…"

"I know… but I'm not lying… I know he knows… I don't know how I know… but I just know… I know he knows… I know he can hear us…"

"WE LOVE YOU…" She screamed unexpectedly into the dark sky that somehow looked like a black hole… "WE'VE ALWAYS LOVED YOU… AND WE'LL LOVE YOU NO MATTER WHAT…"

He held on tight to her… and they both stared at the night sky… They could see his face… him smiling back at them… He hasn't left… He's still there… and that's all that matters…

***

XLIX

Conversation Forty Nine...

It's been 22 days since you've left... It's going to be a month soon and for some reason it seems scary... Me and God... we're still not on talking terms yet... I've heard the phrase that not even Gods can defeat fate... but... I trusted God so much that it hurts to think that God has betrayed me... I've asked so many questions to Him after you left... Why did He take you out of all people...? And this question somehow is at the peak... I still can't understand why He took you from us... But today something happened...

We were talking about our days and your friend told me about a dream he saw... with such clarity... I've read somewhere that if we remember our dreams... then it's a message... and I like to believe it so... Your friend... he saw himself at a place where you both used to spend time together... he was crying in the dream... but he felt a cold hug from behind... and he heard a voice tell him not to be dramatic... It was you... it was your voice he heard... He told me it made him feel some sort of relief... like you're there with him... and my eyes filled up when he told me about it... My eyes are still filled to the brim as I write this to you... knowing full well that I can't ever send this to you... But I know with all my heart that you're reading this... and you're watching over us... at least him... I asked God to give me an explanation... some sort of sign so that I wouldn't lose my complete faith on Him... and for some reason... this dream of his seems like a sign...

I used to wear Bhasma on my forehead... and you've seen it plenty of times... I'm going to do that again... from tomorrow onwards... I'm still angry at Him... I'm still mad at Him... but... I'm willing to give it a shot again... since He gave me a sign... You loved God too... didn't you...? And I know you're with Him... wherever you're... I know that you might not appear in my dreams... but I know you're there... and some day we'll both see you... We might be ugly... and old... with wrinkly face... but you'll still be handsome... you'll still be young... You won't have wrinkles or curved back... and I'm pretty sure you'll tease us when you see us both... and I would do anything to hear that once again...

Anyway... I'm so happy for the sign even though I've tears flowing silently out of my eyes... smudging my kajal... I'm happy to know that you haven't gone... It's never goodbye...

With lots and lots of love...

His tears fell on the scribbled letters... What would he give to see him just one more time... and what would she give to see him more than once... It both made him happy and made him scared... He held the book closer to his chest...

"Don't you dare make it dramatic... friend..."

He heard him whisper through the breeze...

***

L

Conversation Fifty...

She was sitting on the beanbag like usual with her legs above the floor in such a way that he could hold her feet... She was not looking at him... not reading... mainly doing nothing much... Another suspension... he knew... The college she worked in was adamant on it... The first one was her mistake... an ignorant one which they forgave... and she definitely isn't proud of... But the second one was not her fault... actually she hasn't done any of it in the second one... According to the second one, she had yelled at her superior and her teaching methods were extremely inferior... in which case... she hasn't yelled at the superior... in fact she doesn't even talk to her superior... On the second scenario... she had been asking her own students if the portion she was taking was clear over and over and all they did was nod their head... She wasn't a mind reader... she was just a teacher... a human...

"It's fine... We'll get a new job..." he said... He knew this wasn't going to lift her spirit up... Nevertheless... this was all he could offer for now... He gently squeezed her feet...

"I won't... It's a competitive world... I've been writing exams over and over and I've been nothing but a constant failure... I'm stressed out... I'm depressed... I don't even have hope for the future..."

"You'll be fine... You'll qualify the exams..."

"I don't know... I've been trying my best not to count the days... I've been trying my best not to listen to the songs in the playlist I've created for him... and now... on top of it... I don't know why I'm being constantly tested... What lesson am I supposed to learn from it...? For a mistake I never did... for a mistake I never even did..."

"Some people are such..." he began... but he let it fall... There's no explanation needed... She already knew... She wasn't crying... That was a relief... She was simply smiling through her hopelessness... He thought of his friend... He had told him of her first suspension... and he was genuinely surprised... If he had been here... he would have told him about this second one too... and the three of them would have ranted about the teachers there and would have laughed about it... But for both of them... the pain never ceased to exist... It kept going on and on... It was true what the characters in the movies said... Time doesn't heal wounds... it lets you live on with the pain...

"How about I take you out for some hot French fries...? Would that make you feel better...?"

"Yeah... For now..."

"But you're paying... If only my M. A was over...!"

She smiled at him and he smiled back...

***

LI

Conversation Fifty One...

"Do you know something?" she asked out of the blue... Every question from her was always *out-of-the-blue* questions. He was getting quite used to it by now... Questioning the reason behind the question would be pointless... She was never going to tell him that... She was always private of that inner circle where only she existed...

"Hm...?" he hummed absentmindedly... He was listening... listening intently for something important to fall out of her lips... It was one of those faces of hers...

"I guess Plato was right... about Gods dividing us only to spend the rest of our lives searching for our best halves... We search and search and search... and we never find..."

What about him...? He wanted to ask... *Was he not her better half...?* He wanted to continue down this trail of thoughts but she was ready to explain further... or at least that was what her face looked like...

"We fix our life on one person whom we think is our soulmate... and we live with that person... and then one day we realise... we are completely alone in this world... There's no soulmate... There are just a handful of lost souls..."

Lost souls... Lost... wandering souls... Hopeless... The adjectives kept running wild inside his head... *Whom did these adjectives aim to please...? Was it him... his minions at work...? Or were they... his masters...?*

She could see his forehead straining... his eyebrows curving... She almost wished if she could turn the time back and warn herself not to open her mouth... She always made things worse... she always did... She sighed deeply and looked out of the window... at the dark sky... hoping for some written answers to her twisted life... She did not know what more to say... she had no words... Recently she had gone through his voice chats... It has almost been seven months since he has left... their friend... And he left a huge gaping hole in both of them that could not be fixed... If she could see herself from outside her body as if she was watching a movie... she would be the character who has lost everything... who is drunk almost every night... and wake up drunk almost every day... She would be taking drugs and she would be wasted at the side path...

"I think being around people is not what is meant for me..." she said... "I love too much and then I push them off... for fear that they might leave... No human is immortal anyway... and our friend just proved that point to us quite well... Maybe if I let you go now... it would hurt me less and less... Or maybe if I took a dive from this balcony... I might fly... Who knows...!"

She was not drunk... Not to his knowledge... There was not a single bottle of alcohol in their house... And still she managed to get drunk on her own... It was her special skill...

She had mentioned it to him... She could get drunk whenever she wanted to... even in the absence of alcohol in her system... All it took was a great tragedy...

"What would you do if you were living for yourself...?" he asked. He regretted asking it as soon as it was out of his lips and he could not take it back... Not now... Not ever... He knew the answer and dreaded hearing it from her... But it was too late... Their lives won't be the same anymore...

"I don't know... I never knew... I've had no friends to advice me on it... I guess that's what happens to children whose parents interfere too much in their life... even in selecting with whom their daughter should be friends with... I've become dysfunctional... I'm broken in ways I don't know how to repair... I don't think I've anyone outside of you who would actually hold me tight when I cry... No mother... no father... no siblings... no cousins... no friends... just no one... Maybe my name could be taken as a synonym of loneliness... utter loneliness..."

"I don't have any friends..."

"I could name at least two of your friends from the top of my head... You don't know any of mine... I've never talked about anyone... I've had none... I thought I did... but every time I think I did... I push them away... and no one puts up with a high maintenance... I've qualified a bit too much and yet I've nothing... It's the greatest paradox... isn't it...? What we define as success isn't actually success... It's an illusion... and we've been chasing this illusion for far too long and we finally reach there only to realise that we lost things that were real... You can't make friends in your twenties... It's not that age... And I've lost the childhood where I was supposed to have friends... listening blindly to them... I'm broken..."

He looked outside at the dark night sky... There were no answers written down... It only stayed empty like a blackboard... Their childhood was better when there were blackboards and everything changed for the worst when greenboards and whiteboards emerged... Life was perfect with blackboards and all the questions and answers written on it... And now... there were no more answers... only questions...

***

LII

Conversation Fifty Two...

It's been an year now... The months keep flying as if they had somewhere to go... She had become more and more silent... and he... He didn't know what he had become... He was afraid to ask himself... He had been talking to her a lot and nothing had been happening... It was like she had been extinguished all by herself and there was nothing much to reignite her... Not even a spark...

"I guess it's time for me to go..." she said one fine morning out of the blue... "It's time to leave just as how I'd come..."

Don't leave... Please don't leave... I've loved you so much... And I love you so much... Please don't go... Please... I beg you...

"Love alone isn't enough it seems..." she said as if it was too natural... "I need to heal me first... I need to love me first... I need to love me just as how my God loves me... see me just as how He sees me... I deserve at least that... and even more..."

What about me...? Don't I deserve you...? You're leaving me for a small mistake from my part... I love you... I've corrected myself as you'd asked me to... Don't leave me... Please don't leave me... Please... I'm still ready to change... I'll be better... I'll keep my emotions under control... I'll stop depending on you emotionally... I'll listen more... I'll do anything for you...

"You'll find what you deserve... only if you heal... And I want to... I want to stop surviving and start living... I want to love life... I want to see all the colours that I never saw... And I know it's going to be hell just to heal... But it's better than living in lies... At least I'll know that the hell I'm going through is real..."

Who will heal me...? What do I do now...? I'll be alone in this house... Will you come back...? Will you come back if I wait...? Yes... I'll wait... I'll be waiting... I can't live without you... I can't...

"I love you... You taught me what love is... and you taught me how important it is to heal myself... You taught me how to love myself... And I'll always be grateful to you... Thank you... Thank you so much..."

I'll wait... Please come back... Please... This is all a mistake... Please come back... Please...

"I wish you good luck..."

***

And the days and nights crawled along slowly... The house grew darker and colder and lonelier... and the empty shell began sucking him into a black void... She had left a long while ago... He knew... a long while ago before she had told... She wanted to break the cycle that was killing her... and he was happy for her... But he missed her... He loved her... And he still does... He doesn't regret anything... He has done his best... and still she left... He doesn't want to blame her... But at times... he wished if she'd stayed... if she'd asked his help... But she never asked... she never begged... She just left with some words less than a good bye... He deserved more... he knew... But he never told... He only pondered... Was he only that much for her...? He didn't know... and he probably might never...

***